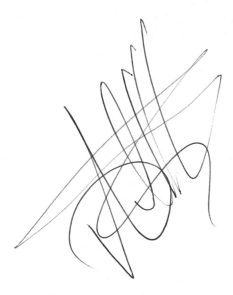

MONSTER MANIA

THE LOVE STORY OF DREAMS

ALISTER MACKINNON

WESTBOW
PRESS®
A DIVISION OF THOMAS NELSON
& ZONDERVAN

WestBow Press books may be ordered through booksellers or by contacting:

WestBow Press
A Division of Thomas Nelson & Zondervan
1663 Liberty Drive
Bloomington, IN 47403
www.westbowpress.com
1 (866) 928-1240

ISBN: 978-1-9736-0421-1 (sc)
ISBN: 978-1-9736-0420-4 (hc)
ISBN: 978-1-9736-0422-8 (e)

Library of Congress Control Number: 2017915888

Print information available on the last page.

WestBow Press rev. date: 11/22/2017

I would like to dedicate my book to my late grandmother who brought me up at a difficult time in my life. A remarkable lady.

ACKNOWLEDGEMENTS

I would like to thank, Michel, Jenny, Nancy, Nicola, and my wife Janet. My software and IT team for their professional and spirited attitude. You were a blessing to work with.

I would like to thank Westbow Press for giving me the opportunity to publish my book with one of the worlds leading publishers.

ACKNOWLEDGMENTS

1

JUST OFF THE WEST COAST OF SCOTLAND
lay the Hebridean Islands, which are rich in fishing,
farming, and deer hunting. The islands' picturesque
mountain ranges created beautiful sunsets to remember, and
the tranquillity of the lochs caused many tourists to come
back.

On an island was a hamlet called Cruach na Moine,
which in Gaelic meant "a peat stack." Peat was the main
source of home fuel for the villagers, particularly during the
long winter season.

The village of Cruach na Moine was scattered. Local
people had crofts (which were small holdings to cultivate)
and livestock such as cows, sheep, ducks, and hens. Many
houses were a mile apart, or in clusters of two or three by
the sea. A small but recognisable school had been also built
by the coast. As a matter of fact, many of the schools on

the island had been built close to the sea because building materials had to come by boat. There were sixteen houses. The village had two churches, a shop cum post office, and a telephone box that served as a lifeline to the locals.

Peat bog where the winter fuel comes from

Church played an important part to the islanders. Most families came to worship every Sunday. Three denominations – the Church of Scotland, the Free Church, and the Presbyterian Church – shared two church buildings. However, this island was not exempt from the temptation of alcohol drinking, which drove some young men to excess. Even though hotels and bars were far away, these men would drive fifteen miles on a Friday or Saturday night to fill their cravings for spirits. Surprisingly, most workers made it to work on Monday, but not all.

One family stood out from the rest.

Close to the creek in a small holding stood a house surrounded with a fence needing repair and a gate that could not close. The home furniture was old, scratched, broken, and handed down from family members and charity.

The outside appearance possibly reflected what was inside. That was where Donald and Mary McPhee lived with their two children: Seonag, which was Gaelic for Joan, aged eight, and her brother Hamish, who was a year older. Both children attended the local primary school, which had an attendance of thirty-five pupils and only one teacher. The couple was well-known by locals and was farther afield for one reason: a serious alcohol problem. This dilemma was reflected in the shabbily dressed children, who were very thin due to poor nutrition and lack of sustenance.

The children were not happy, and neither was the home. A home never was when there was an overindulgence of alcohol. Each child had a room, and the bigger room overlooking the loch was occupied by their parents. It was in the local bar that the children's parents met, decided to get married, and settled in the house next to their grandma, who passed away a few years later.

When the parents were on a bender, the grandmother would look after the children. She had been a great crutch to the couple and to the children. As a godly woman, she would plant godly knowledge of truth into the children's hearts with the hope that one day, when they needed encouragement and support, they would remember what Grandma had taught them and would eventually pass the seed of truth to their own children.

Somehow the children knew they were different from other children. No one came to play with them, and no visitors come to their house except for the postman. All they had were themselves. The children shared their sorrow with each other, and no one could untangle their love for one another.

Alcohol brought arguments over money and bills into the house. Donald had been laid off from work because of his drinking. Income was difficult because he had to rely on benefits and casual work. Life existed without any vision for their future and the future of the children.

Going to school was not something they always looked forward to, because children can be so cruel. Oftentimes their parents' drinking sprees were widely spoken of, and the school playground was not a safe haven for such news either. For Seonag and Hamish, class break time became a dreadful period. They found it easier to accept the stories than to fight back, because they knew that the rumours were true. What a great relief whenever classes resumed, so that they could shut their ears to taunts!

Rex, the dog, was there to make them smile after a long, dismal day at school. Even though he was old and inactive, he was their faithful friend. He was an old collie that had performed a good share of service to the family.

There were times that life was unbearable for Seonag and Hamish, when their parents were sobering up because money was short. The hangovers were as bad as the drinking binges.

They missed their grandma and spoke often about her. She was the only person to whom their parents would listen. Now she was gone, and no one was brave enough to point the finger and give them some home truths. Granny had tried to guide them in the right direction, but all her advice fell on the deaf ears of their parents. The children remembered the excitement in going to their grandma's house with candy and chocolate stashed for them, to take their minds off the situation at home.

2

ONE EVENING, AS HAMISH WAS preparing his homework for the next day, he noticed his sister was very quiet and engrossed in a newspaper article. The paper was several days old and handed down from the neighbours. She never read daily newspapers, only comic strips. Today, however, she read it in a way that she didn't want to be noticed. But Hamish noticed his sister tear a page from the rest of the paper, fold it, and insert it into her school bag before marching off to her bedroom.

That evening, Hamish entered his sister's room while she was asleep to try to find the cutting. However, he noticed something peculiar. She had the article gripped tightly in her hand. Hamish knew if he tried to remove it, she would wake. He switched off her light, shut the door, and left for his own room to sleep.

Something is going on with my sister. Maybe Dad has been

in trouble and is in the papers, Hamish surmised while he lay on his bed. Why was she keeping it from him? They shared everything, so why keep a secret from her brother now? She knew they needed each other, and if Dad was in trouble, she should share it with him. Hamish was upset, and it took him a while before he dozed off.

The next day, they went to school and did their normal routine. That night, while his sister was doing some chores at home, he sneaked into her room and searched for that article, but to no avail. He searched her schoolbag and through her music records, but still there was no sign.

In the evening, Seonag could hardly stop looking at the clock. Her brother was quite sure that she was not expecting anyone to visit them. At nine thirty, she flipped the television to channel 4. This was quite a normal thing. Seonag had no great interest in movies, news programs, or even pop music. While Seonag was busy preparing to record the program that night, Hamish was on the sofa, completely puzzled with what was going on with his sister. *Why? Never has she done this before,* he thought.

Sometimes when they went out, they would record TV programmes, but nothing was important enough to video it while they were in the house. Hamish stopped doing his homework, slid down on the couch, and picked up a comic, pretending to read it. As the documentary programme started, he was even more confused. It showed images of underground sewers in the Eastern Block. It showed children living among rats. Some of the children showed the scars of what these beasts had done to them, and many of them were sick.

Why in the world does Seonag want to watch this – and video it as well? She was so engrossed in watching that she barely noticed her brother was watching too. The presenter of the programme was in the sewers, speaking to some of the children, and he asked what brought them to this position. Many had sad stories of being separated from their families due to war or poverty, and others were due to a family breakdown caused by alcohol.

"I left home to get away from my parents," remarked a boy. Surprisingly, he looked better off than the rest of the children. He looked healthy and clean, and he had good manners.

The presenter asked him, "How long have you been in the sewers?"

The boy replied, "Six years, but now I live in the orphanage of dreams. I come here to help my old friends." The presenter asked to see the place where he used to live, and to speak to some of the other children who had survived.

Then they interviewed a man who did not have an Odessa accent. He indicated that he came to help those who were less fortunate than himself, and he began to tell his story.

He had been an alcoholic for thirty years, lost his business, was given only two years to live due to bad health, and had liver cirrhosis aided by alcohol. He experienced being homeless and unable to keep a job. He suffered from a mental condition and had to be in mental hospitals over thirty times for treatments related to alcohol abuse. He underwent detox and rehabilitation programmes several times.

The man explained that one night, while drinking in a bar, he felt the power of God, and this changed his life. On that night, he found himself walking out of the bar to the nearby local church. Months later, he met a beautiful woman who became his wife. She was a loving and a caring person. For the first time in his life, he'd found a home. His life changed, his health improved, his debts were paid back, and he gained respect from people who hadn't given it to him before. Eventually he managed to get a job on the oil rigs, which he loved.

But once again, his life took another twist. His wife was taken into hospital and died after a short illness. In fact, during this period his mum also died, as well as his best friend. At this point, he had all the excuses in the world to go back to his old life. But then he said to himself, "Going back is not an option." Loneliness forced him to make something worthwhile with his life and help others. He decided to come to Odessa to help for a period, when he could afford it.

The presenter asked him where he came from. "The Western Isles of Scotland," he answered.

By this time, Hamish was as engrossed in the programme as Seonag was. The documentary showed the orphanage of dreams where the children lived. Around forty children lived in a beautiful building with a garden. Although the surrounding areas were rough, the conditions within the orphanage were so much different. Some bedrooms could take up to six kids. There was a large playing room, a large kitchen, and a lounge with a coloured television. What stood out were the shining faces of the children, so happily loved and well cared for. The staff at the orphanage of dreams were dedicated and loving.

The filming crew spoke to the boy they met in the sewers earlier and asked him what happen beyond the orphanage. He said his parents realised what it cost them by drinking too much, and they were now attending a church and various rehabilitation programmes.

The most interesting part was that he received a visit from his parents once a fortnight. He went on to say that he hoped that one day, they could be a family again. Maybe by that time, he would be able to get a job to support his family and make a career for himself.

Tears filled Seonag's eyes and ran down her cheeks. Her brother saw this, his eyes also filled with tears. The final part showed the Scotsman playing well-known Scottish music, with the children dancing and showing the warm atmosphere that could be felt hundreds of miles away in Cruach an Moine.

As the programme came to an end and they switched off the TV, their parents arrived from the bar in a state of drunkenness. Fear gripped the children again as they were questioned why they were still up. The children disappeared to their rooms.

In his bedroom, Hamish was filled with unanswered thoughts about those sad children who were left to look after themselves. *How could their parents allow such to happen to their children?* he thought. *Are we like that? Are we any better off than them?* He cried from his heart with pain, first for his parents and then for him and Seonag. It was very hard to sleep when he was in this state.

This was a mystery to poor Hamish. He then thought about himself and compared his lifestyle with theirs. His thoughts reflected the happiness in the orphanage.

The children were well cared for and had everything they needed. He paused for a moment. Then he jumped out of his bed to visit his sister. He opened his sister bedroom door and noticed that she was fast asleep, clutching the newspaper cutting. This time he managed to get it out of her hand and tiptoe back to his own room. He looked at the crumbled cutting, and to his amazement, he noticed the article was based on the documentary he had just seen on TV. What was the connection? Why the great interest? Hamish took the article back to his sister's room, left it on the bed, and hurried back to his own room.

He still found it hard to get to sleep. He tossed and turned for a while. He decided to splash cold water on his face in the bathroom and went back to his room. Was his sister planning to run away? With these deep thoughts, he fell asleep.

Hamish was woken up early the morning by his dad's rough voice, who was still half drunk and smelled badly of old beer and sweat. This made Hamish leave the room quickly and get into the bathroom. Very soon Hamish and his sister set off together for school, which was a short distance from where they lived. Not a word was spoken between the two – neither any mention of the weather nor the programme they had watched the night before.

When they met up at school break, they spoke only about their homework and schoolwork. At four o'clock, school was done, and they walked home. They enjoyed each other's company and knew so much about each other that at times, they felt they were buddies instead of brother and sister. Life at home made them this way. The afternoon sunshine was warm, although summer would soon be ending and the autumn was fast approaching. They made the best of the fine weather.

3

AS THEY CAME CLOSER TO THEIR HOME, they noticed a black vehicle parked at their gate. It looked like an official car with no markings on it. Seonag and Hamish daren't go inside, and instead they went unto an adjacent shed close to the living room. The living room window was open, probably to allow the smell of alcohol to leave the room.

Hamish signalled to Seonag to be quiet as he tried to figure out how many people were inside and why they'd came. At first he could make out that there were two women, but their father's voice seemed to drown the conversation. At last his father quietened for a few moments, and Hamish could hear the voice of another man. The gist of what the unidentified man said was that their parents had been reported for leaving their children alone, and for being unfit to look after them even when they were at home.

A cold shiver went through the children as the man explained the children would be taken into social care for a period of time until their parents were in a position to look after them. Hamish and Seonag tiptoed from the shed down the path and away from the house. After an hour, they saw two women and a tall gentleman leave their house with briefcases in their hands, where the future of the family possibly lay.

Even though life was in a mess, they loved their parents. No matter how many times the cupboards were bare and the larder was empty, they managed to get by. They were not the worst off children in the world. Seeing that documentary made them grateful.

However, for Seonag and Hamish, being taken into care was close to the bottom rung of the ladder. Many things could happen, and they may never see their parents again – or each other.

As the two children sat by the small stream, a few ducks swam by gracefully. Just when they thought that life could not get any worse, it did. The breakup of the family was as bad as it could get. It was the fear of being separated from each other that they dreaded the most. For them, it would be unthinkable. They couldn't live without each other. They were like two peas in a pod. They knew that in this situation, many families would never get back together. In many cases, both parents and the children grew apart. There would be many feelings: anger, rejection, depression, and perhaps turning to alcohol, which had originally separated them.

It was time to face their parents at home. They crept up

the path and took off their boots by the door. They tried to be on their best behaviour and made their way to the kitchen. In these rural areas, many families spent most of their time in the kitchen because the stove kept them warm. The living room was mostly used only for visitors, as it had been today.

The parents said nothing to them; for once, they were not arguing and seemed quite normal. It was easy to do that for short spells. Their mother was making homemade soup, and their father was peeling potatoes. Should this had happened many years before, they could have avoided the scenario they had witnessed earlier on – and even now, it was possibly too late.

After washing the dishes, their parents told them that they could play outside. That never happened during school days. They were asked to be in at half past eight. Their parents went to the living room to talk. Two hours outside with a full stomach? Was this a lull before the storm?

After sitting down on a little bench, Seonag brought up the issue of what they had seen on the TV programme. She took out the newspaper cutting that corresponded with the documentary. Hamish attentively listened to his sister as she stammered, trying to speak quickly and hold back her tears. "Could you please slow down?" he muttered.

But she got more emotional and fearful for the two of them. "Something has to be done," she said. She couldn't bear to stay and let their lives go further down to the gutter. "Listen to me," she begged Hamish.

He put his arms round her as he did on many other occasions and said, "I'm listening."

Then there was a pause. Seonag looked at her brother. "Where is Odessa?" she asked.

Hamish closed his eyes as his sister laid before him a plan that was beyond any fantasy story. It could end up fatal for them both. A foreign country with a language barrier and with little money ... the list went on.

Hamish listened quietly for once. He did not say that she was stupid or had gone crazy, but he was frozen into silence. He had no words to answer the question of his sister. He did not find it a normal question to ask, and it could not be answered in a few words. As he looked at her, he heard his mother calling them home. Surprisingly, hot drinks were waiting for them inside, and after that they went to bed. Hamish found it hard to answer his sisters question, because this question had to be answered without hurting his sister, who was more stressed than he was.

In his room, Hamish put all these to the test. What if she had a point, and they made it to the orphanage of their dreams in Odessa? He then looked at the negative side: the strange and bad people that they could run into. They would be vulnerable to the outside world. Then he looked at the transport, passports, clothes, food, lodgings, and so on. The idea was crazy and unthinkable. Or was it?

A few days went by, and their home life was good. Had their parents changed for the best? The result of the visitors' meeting would be known by the end of the month.

Thursday came, and nothing changed; it was business as usual. The money came, the parents cleaned up and went to the bar, and the children were left on their own to look after each other. The hours of waiting took a toll on the children. They knew that the bar closed at ten at night, and the hope of a lift home was better than spending what money they had left on a taxi.

The door swung open: it was their parents. They were more sociable to each other and to the children than usual. Instead of the raised voice Donald usually had, he burst into a loud and uncontrollable crying full of remorse. Mary was more subtle and told him to be quiet, as if to keep this latest problem from the children. Unknown to them, the children already knew. Donald cried himself to sleep.

As a year older than Seonag, Hamish felt the responsibility for the welfare of his sister.

He slipped onto his knees as he remembered what his grandma had once told him. "When in trouble, bring it to God in prayer," she would say. He did so with simple words that only God could understand. After praying, he sat on the edge of his bed, gazing up at the sky with the moonlight beaming through the clouds.

It was so beautiful as he gazed at the galaxies thousands of miles away. Down here in his home, he felt as though he was stuck in a corner. Many young people found themselves in this position, and many times the outside world did not see it, but as children got older, these circumstances did affect them in many ways. In this case, there seemed to be no way out. Or was there? Was his sister showing a backbone and wanting to attempt an almost impossible task?

Was he on the verge of agreeing with her? If he agreed, there would no way back. He glanced at the clock, and it was late, ten minutes to midnight. He slipped into his pyjamas that grandma had bought him and slowly crept to his sister's room to waken her. As he approached her room, he could hear a sound coming from within. She was counting the few coins that she kept in an empty jam jar. This coins had taken her the eight years of her life to save. When she noticed him, it was too late to hide them.

Without any hesitation, she looked at her brother and asked, "How much have you got saved?"

"Have you got enough to go first class?" Hamish asked her teasingly. Seonag had counted all her money, which came to seven pound and ten shillings – a huge amount for a little girl. Hamish indicated that he had nine pounds. He sat on the edge of the bed, looked at his sister, and used three words that would change their lives forever. "Let's do it!" With a high-five and a clenched fist, the deal was done.

4

WHEN THE MORNING APPROACHED, they got up. Mother prepared toast, boiled eggs, and tea. Without a doubt, she loved their children, but her love was divided between alcohol and her children. With still bits of eggs on their faces, they left home with an unusual swagger, as if the world was their oyster. Well, it was, but going back to school was another thorn in their flesh.

But it's going to be different this time, Hamish told himself. He wasn't going to take this bullying any longer. He would rather go home beat up, bruised, and defeated than continue being a wimp.

As Hamish tried to pass one of the leading bullies, the bully pushed Hamish to the ground. Hamish quickly stood up, pulled the boy from his pack of mates. and punched him twice in quick succession, which resulted in the bully landing flat on his back. The rest of his pals, who normally enjoyed seeing Hamish being on the ground, backed off and scurried away to their classes.

Hamish stood over the boy and offered him his hand, which the boy accepted. Then they both went to their classes.

Seonag was caught up in a similar situation by the girls who pulled her pigtails. It was easy to take the beating, but it would happen again and again. Seonag was pushed to the ground, but she quickly retaliated by kneeing one of the girls, which was met with a loud scream. She then caught her bully in the ribs with her schoolbag, which had her rolling around on the ground. Again, the rest of the pack backed off and went to their classrooms. Seonag stayed put and sent a warning to the other girls that they should never pull her pigtails again.

By lunchtime the whole school had knowledge of what had happened in the morning. At lunch break, the two children enjoyed a bully-free afternoon In fact, some children saw them as heroes; not all children were caught up with this type of caper. It was a day that Seonag and Hamish would not forget. As they left school later that day, they felt like normal children and made their way home.

When they approached their home, the black car was back. This time they did not hide but came in and went to their rooms. This was the manner in this area: if someone came to a house, the children would go to their rooms and wait to be called down. A knock on their bedroom door from their mother told them that there were some people who wanted to speak to them. They had never spoken to strangers before.

A younger woman was doing all the writing while the other woman, who was in her mid-fifties, and the tall man of about forty-five years old smiled at them.

"Have you had a good day at school today?" they asked.

"Yes, we had. Thank you," the children replied.

The conversation became serious, and the visitors informed Hamish and Seonag that the authorities were aware that they were being left behind by their parents and exposed to an alcohol environment. The officials said that this could not be tolerated by the authorities and that they were going through a code of practice that would help both the parents and the children. They believed their mum and dad needed professional help for their addiction, and the good news was that a place was available in ten days' time.

A decision was being made for the children to be taken into care for a short period. This would happen in just over a week's time. The strange people concluded by telling the whole family that it was very possible that all could go back to living normally again, but it often didn't happen that way. As the officers prepared to leave, they told the children what they should bring with them when they went into care.

Seonag spoke up. "What about Rex?" The look on the male officer's face showed no sympathy towards her question, and she did not get an answer. Rex was a faithful dog not only to the children but to the parents. As the car whizzed off, the parents tried to make light of it, saying that it would only be for a short while, and when they came home, their father would get a job. Then they could maybe move away for a fresh start. But in many cases moving away isn't always the answer, sadly many take there addiction problem with then.

Can we go out and play outside?" the children asked.

"Sure, you can," permitted by their parents as a peace offering.

The children made their way to their favourite bench. Hamish had a pencil and paper to start making their plans to leave. They looked at each other and said, "Thursday will be the perfect day!" This was the usual day the postman brought the benefits to their parents, who would then catch the bus to the village to religiously spend their money.

5

HAMISH, YOU CAN BE THE BANKER, and I will look out after the rations," blurted Seonag. They smuggled some food to the shed to hide for their journey. Hamish had a small rucksack, and Seonag had a Spiderman bag. They always got scones from a neighbour who knew that by Wednesday, the cupboards would be bare. The scones were a blessing to the children, filled with treacle that filled their stomachs.

On Wednesday they put a third of the scones, along with soap, toothpaste, a towel, toothbrushes, and a change of clothes, in their stash.

This filled their bags to capacity. As the weekend drew closer, the children felt sad that this decision had to be made. Hamish had a map he'd borrowed from the school about Odessa. The children continued to go to school, which was now bearable, but for them it was too late.

Thursday morning approached, and the children got up as normal. What they were doing to their parents may hurt them, but this worked both ways. That day they decided not to go to school, but they sat on a hill that was close to the road. They saw the postman cycling up to the cottage, carrying the money that would give their parents the substance they craved. Then they saw their parents leave their home and boarded the bus. As the bus went out of sight, there was nothing in the world that the children wanted more dearly than to be a family again. But at this moment, they had decided to go their own way.

With the bus out of sight, the coast was clear – it was now time for action. Hamish filled his rucksack with the necessary things they would require for the trip and the little food they had, which was enough for only a couple of days. That was as far as they would project in their minds; beyond that was a mystery.

As they prepared to leave, they looked around their home. Then they looked out the window to see the ocean and the hills in the background. As Hamish glanced in the mirror, he could see the sadness in his face as he prepared to leave his home, maybe for the last time. His sister tidied up her bedroom. The house was filled with the smell of the carpet, which was stained with beer and cigarettes. This existence was barely a home. At the end of that day, their parents would return again, and the cycle would go on and on.

Hamish put his rucksack on his back. They thought of leaving a note for their parents, but they couldn't come to the point of saying why they were leaving or where they were going. They had been brought up by their grandma to not tell lies, so it was better for them to not say anything at all. Rex the dog was aware that he wasn't going with them for a walk, so he made no attempt to wag his tail and get excited.

Seonag picked up the article that was in the paper and put it in her purse. All girls have purses whether or not they have money.

The bus was due within an hour, which gave them time to have their last meal at home. They shared a tin of beans and some toast, which for them was a proper meal. Time flew by, and they could see the bus a mile away. They shut their front door for the last time, with Rex accompanying them to the gate. He would not go any further unless he was called upon. It seemed that even Rex knew that this was not going to be the case.

The bus pulled up, and they jumped on and paid the fare to the bigger village, where they would be able to get a bus that would go to Inverness. They had only enough money to go halfway, and their tickets indicated that they would get as far as Loch Ness. "We will spend the night at Loch Ness, and tomorrow will look after itself."

As the bus took off, they watched the fields where they used to run and play, as well as the burns in which they had fished. The bus turned a corner, and their home life was behind them. They nodded off for a bit, and within thirty minutes they alighted from the bus.

They waited about fifty minutes to board the next bus, which would take them off the island they loved so much. This time they were leaving it for a better life, not just an existence. The bus approached the ferry that would take them to the mainland, and in a few short minutes, they were off the island and moving farther away from Cruach na Moine.

There were tourists on the bus from all over the world to see the beautiful sceneries of Scotland, and very soon they were on a winding road. In a short time, they were at Loch Ness. The bus pulled up at a lay-by, and the children gathered their belongings making sure they left nothing behind. The children got off the bus, and within seconds the door shut. The bus sped away towards a winding corner. The sound of the engine got quieter as the bus disappeared out of sight.

The children attempted to cross the road at a time when it was very busy, due to the busy end of the tourist season. Just like many other children, they headed for the lakeside, their mission was to camp for the night and prepare for the very long journey. On the shores of Loch Ness, their tummies were giving them signals that required attention. Just like any other child on the shore, the children picked up several small flat stones, skipped them across the top of the lake, and watched who could make the stone jump the most times. It was a very common game amongst young children in the islands, where facilities for sports were not accessible; they had to do with what was available.

It was quite easy to get bored at the loch, especially if one was not caught up in the euphoric phobia of the Loch Ness monster. These children weren't. What was important to them tonight was their survival kit in two small bags, which were only enough for few days. A sleeping place would have to be found before darkness came. This was still a while away; in summer there was little darkness, and in winter there was little light.

Weather in the highlands was unpredictable and could change very quickly from brilliant sunshine to pouring rain. The first night below the starry sky in the open air was an experience for those much older; it meant far less to the younger ones who were about to have this experience. Most tourists were returning to their hotels or campsites and getting ready for their evening meal, relaxing and reviewing pictures they had taken that day.

This wasn't the case for the children. Seonag pulled a thin blanket from the bag and laid it on the uneven ground. Hamish gathered a few dry sticks to make a small fire. Unknown to his sister, he'd brought a box of matches, which was forbidden to all children because of the dangers they may cause. In the end, she was happy to get a little heat. Hamish dealt with the supper, which consisted of tinned sausages and beans, soup, a banana, and a glass of warm milk that had been exposed to the sun all day.

"Not the worst menu in the world," they said. Many children would have been happy with half that portion for the whole day. They ate quite quickly because this was their first snack since breakfast.

For a moment, it was every child's dream to camp beside the famous lake. Seonag opened the one-man sleeping bag for both of them. There were no adults to boss them about; they could come and go as they pleased. Everything was free. What a deal! But the sun would not last all night. The darkness would creep in, and the wind would start to rise.

Seonag crawled under the sleeping bag. Hamish made sure the fire would not spread or burn the hillside. Hamish slipped off his shoes and crawled beside his sister in silence. Both of them were in deep thoughts as to why they were in this position.

Hamish glanced at a bush that was nearby where they were sleeping. Embedded in this bush was an empty beer bottle, which may have been swept by the wind or were maybe the leftovers of a party. He knew the damage the contents of that bottle had done to his family, and many families throughout the world.

"What are you thinking, Hamish?" asked Seonag.

"That bottle is bothering me," he replied. "It reminds me of our parents."

Seonag saw it, jumped out of the sleeping bag, grabbed the bottle, and threw it out of their sight. "There's where it belongs," she said, smiling at Hamish. It was thrown with anger. The anger was directed not at the bottle but at the dangerous contents that had been devoured some time ago. She lay back down again to get some rest, and Hamish said a prayer that their grandma had taught them.

They looked across the lake and watched the stunning reflection of the moon and the stars, "Maybe Grandma is looking down on us, Hamish."

They laughed as if they didn't have a care in the world.

They both watched the sun go down, as if the world was being switched off for a period of time. There were no sheep bleating, no seagulls flying, and very little traffic. Very soon both of the children slipped into unconsciousness.

It was sad that alcohol had driven two young children to such a sense of despair that they were willing to go to any length for freedom. At that moment, the children had their first alcohol-free evening, and they went to sleep knowing they would not be wakened by arguments or shouting ... or would they?

6

A NEW DAY WAS DAWNING. THERE WAS no running to the bathroom to clean their teeth, and no cereal and milk for today. They wouldn't be picking up their school bags, and neither would they be going to school. This was the start of a new adventure. It was not a fantasy or a dream, but reality. There were many times in life that people believed their dreams and their hopes would never come to pass, but Seonag and Hamish had put their money where their mouth was – well, the little money they had.

The sky showed glimpses that the sun would be appearing once again across the horizon, where a mixture of colours showed the beauty of a mid-summer dawn. There were no ripples on the water because the wind had decided to blow itself out. In the world of sleep, the children were not aware of the beauty of the morning that was beginning by the loch side. As they tossed and turned, Hamish heard a loud roar, which startled him at first, but he soon turned back over to sleep.

A short time later, they were both awakened by a cry that sounded like a bear in pain. The noise seemed to be coming from a short distance from where they had set up camp. They had many rude awakenings in their short life, but none like this. The children jumped up from their makeshift bed because they were already dressed apart from their shoes and jackets. Their first instinct was to run, but to where? They ran from where they believed the noise was coming. Unfortunately, with the many bushes, nettles, and heather, it was quite difficult for the children to make a quick getaway. They crept close to each other, not saying a word but breathing heavily. This was unnatural, uncharted waters and was not part of the script. They were aware that they would encounter many problems, but they did not expect it to be so close to home.

The children, gripped with a new fear they hadn't experienced before, tried to get as far from the area as they could. They were unfamiliar with the lay of the land and were not aware of the hurdles. Getting away when one was in a hurry was difficult. But as they paused for a moment to catch their breath, the cry had changed its pitch to one of pain more than an intention to hurt someone.

Behind a small dune, the children clung to each other. At this moment they were more concerned about their safety than being inquisitive and nosey. They watched the sky brighten to the point where they could clearly recognise each other. Now was the time for the decision to be made;

they had to make up their minds very quickly about what their next move would be.

A third loud scream came from the same area as the first two. This showed whatever was causing this commotion was stationary and not moving, but this time the sound was a little weaker than before.

Was someone hurt? Was it a wild animal caught in a fence? Although Seonag and Hamish were on the shore of Loch Ness, nothing went through their minds regarding the Loch Ness monster or any of the stories that filled the hearts of millions who travelled here in the hope of getting a glimpse.

Even at this time in the morning, their minds were still confused while trying to waken up. They looked at each other to determine who was going to come up with the next move. Their minds began to go towards investigating the situation rather than running farther away. They had to investigate in a way that would not endanger their lives.

In the last twenty-four hours, so much had happened, and now they were in the grip of an important decision. They crawled on their hands and knees between the small clusters of heather and headed into a dried-up brook. As they pushed the bracken from their faces, they continued to crawl nearer to the vicinity of from where the sound had been coming. It may have been ten minutes since the last loud roar.

When a clearing became visible, they could see several feet in front of them. It was time to take a break to gather their thoughts, but just as they took a breather, a thundering roar came, this time as if it was very close to them. In fact it was so close that the ground and the bushes shook like a storm.

Instead of running, the children hid in the bushes to prevent themselves from getting hurt. The dust settled once again, and there was calm, but there was also an expectancy that another outburst would come. As they listened and waited, they could hear what seemed to be a groan every few minutes. The children had come to a point where they could no longer be kept hidden, and it was time to eyeball whatever was there.

But why was it there, and why the painful groans? Was it stuck in a bog? It was not unusual for animals to fall into a bog, although the area was fairly dry. This time of the year, most bogs were dried up, but this was an area about which they knew little.

It was time for Hamish to lead the way over the hill. They climbed by pulling themselves up but not standing up, which made it very hard.

They made their way over the hill without a word or sound, and all of a sudden their eyes were fixed on a large creature. They were too close to be able to make out how big it really was. From the children's point of view, the head was not visible, only the body, which looked as if it was similar to the skin of a crocodile but not so rough. The skin shone in the rising sun, which reflected like a mirror. The children felt that they were being watched by the creature even though there were no signs of the upper part of the body. It was as if they had met a mountain that moved.

The children were amazed by what they saw. They were

in no position to investigate, and they stood motionless and almost in tears No movement came from the creature. All of a sudden, the creature moved, and they could make out the neck and head. They then saw a face that looked sad; the eyes did not blink, but their colours were of the rainbow and changed all the time. The nose was strange. It looked like a highland coo with no horns. The mouth looked weather-beaten with a redness, and as they looked at the teeth, they noticed they were like tusks of ivory.

The children saw two huge flippers that were similar to large paddles. Within it were large jets, possibly to help in the water and to give speed. The flippers at the front were much larger, but only one was visible to the children. It was as if the creature was leaning on the other flipper for some reason. The creature once again moved, but unknown to Hamish and Seonag, it appeared as if it had managed to turn to face them. There was very little happening that brought fear to the children, which was very unusual.

Then there was another groan from the creature. Although the face was strange, it seemed very much in pain. However, it did not look angry. "Are those tears coming down from its eyes?" Seonag muttered. She took a small hanky and made a move to give it to the creature.

"No. That won't help," Hamish stammered.

To their great amazement, they then noticed smoke coming from the nostrils of the creature, like a foaming fog – not like the Scottish fog, which was wet and dreary, but much brighter. Within a short time, the fog surrounded the creature and the children. The children could no longer see the loch, the sky, or even the hills. It was as if there was no way out. The children were not afraid, and neither did they feel they were being threatened by this sad creature.

This is where the children came into contact with the monster on the shores of Loch Ness.

Inside this fog was like a starry sky, and there was a warmth that had a feeling of no danger. The children could see that the hair of this creature had been sort of ginger or reddish at one time. The hair ran down the large neck, and as it reached farther down the neck, the lighter the colour got until it was almost grey. It was hard to put an age on this creature, but it wasn't born yesterday. On the other hand, it could be hundreds of years old. The children admired the features of the creature: the moving eyes that could see all around, the nostrils that made the wonderful fog, and that Highland smile, showing its teeth that looked like ivory tusks. The children noticed there did not seem to be ears, but slants that were like gills that opened and closed as the body breathed. The back was made up like a small hill, tapering like a ski slope. With all these features, one could only fall in love from a child's prospective.

Although the creature was obviously in a lot of pain, the children could not see anything that would indicate there was an injury. Hamish started to look around the creature to see for himself how large it was. The children also wondered what it was doing on land. By this time, the creature had moved into a position where they could see the flipper that had been hidden before. There was something strange about this flipper. It didn't look right, and there seemed to be blood on the heather next to it.

Hamish summoned his sister to his side, and she agreed there was something very far wrong. They decided to go a little closer, knowing that this large animal could turn around and crush them to death at any point. Still, they were without fear as they strived to get closer to this large flipper. To their horror, they saw a large anchor embedded in the creature's chest, and a large chain was entangled round about the flipper.

Amazingly, a huge creature like this, so strong and powerful, could be brought to a standstill with this contraption. The children examined the anchor and the chain, which had cut into its flesh and caused the pain and discomfort. Although Hamish was just a boy, he knew something about boats, anchors, and chains because he had seen people mooring boats near his home back on the island. He also knew that the chain was engaged to the anchor by a shackle, and in order to separate one from the other, a gadget called a shifter would have to be used.

How could this young man tell this creature that there was a solution to ease her pain? He would need to travel to Drumnadrochit, the nearest village, to get a twelve-inch shifter, as well as a can of WD-40 to release the shackle that was being held by a bolt. Once the bolt was removed, the anchor should separate from the chain.

The creature watched the children. There was an awareness that a release from the pain was in the hands of siblings. Seonag cried at the sight of the flipper, which was mangled up in the large, heavy chain. Was there a fight against time? Was this a mammal? Fear began to creep into the children – fear that the creature may die.

How would they get out of the fog? Hamish decided to do the speaking. He spoke as if he was speaking to a neighbour and explained to the creature, in his best English, that in order to be released from the anchor and chain, they would require a mechanical tool and a can of liquid. Getting these things was a tall order. As he explained, the creature looked at him with no body movement.

At that moment, Seonag piped up with a last resort by using her native language, Gaelic, which was commonly spoken in the Highlands and Hebrides of Scotland. The creature nodded in agreement that the required gadget had to be found away from the shore.

"I will go get the shifter so that she can be freed," Hamish said. "But how will I get out of the fog?" The creature understood him, and within seconds, it blew a hole in the fog to allow Hamish to leave. Seonag realised that they would be separated, being on the shores of Loch Ness with a huge creature and no one to protect her was the last thing she wanted, but there was no other option available.

Hamish disappeared through the fog, which then closed behind him as if the hole had never happened. Once outside, to his amazement Hamish could see no mist; the loch side was normal. He could not see his sister, but in good faith he believed she was there alone with the creature. He trusted that the creature would not harm his sister.

Hamish started the long walk from the loch side and headed to the main road and the garage, which would take an hour. The road had no pavement and was getting very busy with morning traffic because it was still summer.

7

THE WINDY ROAD WITH NO PAVEMENT made it difficult to walk. After an hour of walking, a motorist slowed down. An elderly couple asked if he needed a ride. Hamish told them yes, but only to the garage at Drumnadrochit. The elderly woman was very chatty, and she spoke about the lovely weather as many would, as well as what a young boy was doing walking on his own so early in the morning.

Hamish was taught by his grandmother not to tell lies, but when he mentioned he was going to the garage to get a twelve-inch shifter and WD-40, the elderly couple looked at each other and smiled. Hamish knew that they did not believe him.

"Why do you need this contraption?" the old man asked.

"To set a great monster free from an anchor and chain that are wrapped round her flipper. She is in terrible pain and discomfort," Hamish replied. "In fact, my sister is with the monster and is waiting for me."

Upon hearing this, the elderly woman scolded the young man for how he was abusing their kindness by telling them a pack of lies.

The husband found it more amusing and struggled to drive as he was doubled up with laughter. "Don't be silly, young man. There is no such thing as a monster!"

Hamish looked straight ahead with a smirk on his face. They pulled up outside the garage. "Thank you very much," he politely said to the elderly couple.

Hamish fumbled in his small pocket for the little money he had. The last thing he'd expected to buy with his money was a mechanical tool and a can of WD-40. The WD-40 would allow the threads to be loosened on the shackle that bound together the anchor and chain. Once the fluid got into the threads and the bolt, it would make it much easier to be loosened and would allow the creature to get free. This fluid had been well-known for many years. It was found often in workshops, in garages, in the trunk of a car or, in many outdoor sheds because it had many functions. The downside was that it was quite expensive, especially for poor Hamish.

He pushed open the door of the small store, which sold emergency goods and petrol. He joined the line to be serviced and could see the WD-40 on display at a price that would leave him totally broke. This money was supposed to last much longer, but Hamish knew little about the big, wide world with all its pitfalls.

"Can I help you, young man?" asked the middle-aged woman behind the till.

"Yes. Could I please speak to the mechanic?" Hamish answered. He had a plan that may save him money.

The woman was startled for a moment, but it sounded quite normal, even at his young age. She directed Hamish to a large shed behind the store.

"Thank you," Hamish replied. He made his way through a narrow, winding walkway that was possibly between the home of the owner and the store. He entered unseen and could see no one, so he wandered around, looking at stripped car engines, parts of trucks, and bikes. As he was becoming engrossed, he heard a shout.

"What do you want?" Hamish was startled by the manner of the voice. A man of around forty-five years of age came towards him. He was red-faced, looked mean, and smelled of alcohol. Again the man asked what Hamish wanted, but in a more downbeat manner when he saw it was a young boy. Although he did not recognise him, he may have known his father; in local communities, everybody knew each other – and very often their business.

Hamish asked if he could borrow a twelve-inch shifter and some WD-40. The mechanic looked at him in surprise at the request. "What in the world do you need it for?" the man asked.

This time Hamish was a bit more cautious of what to say. He did not want to repeat what he'd told the elderly woman in the car. He told the truth up to a point: an anchor and chain needed to be separated, and he needed the shifter to release the chain from the anchor.

"Can you do it by yourself? Who is with you?" the mechanic asked him.

"My sister is with me," he answered without saying that his sister was younger than him.

The mechanic, like many in the Highlands and Islands, was kind-hearted and willing to give a hand whenever possible – and often there may be a financial gain for the effort! The mechanic introduced himself as Lachie, and Hamish told him his name.

Lachie the mechanic went to his bench, which was covered with tools, and after a short search he pulled up a twelve-inch shifter. Hamish had never used one but had watched other people use them. Lachie assumed there was a boat involved. "So, where is the boat?" he asked Hamish. Again Hamish confused him by saying that there was no boat.

By this time Lachie was getting inquisitive and decided to accompany Hamish to the lochside. At least he would have a better chance of retrieving his tool by going with Hamish. Lachie told his workmates that he was leaving for a while. Hamish was led to an old van, and within minutes they were on the winding road back to the shore of Loch Ness.

All this gave Hamish a headache, and he thought, *What if he comes with me and discovers the creature? Oh, boy. What if this is the Loch Ness monster?*

Time was not on Hamish's side, and as they approached the area, he gazed across the loch side. Everything looked so calm. Hamish pointed to a signpost that indicated a slip road to the loch side. Eventually they reached a man-made parking spot. They both left the van and made their way down the grassy slope until they reached the shingles by the lake. Although Hamish could not see where his sister was or where the creature was, he had a good idea.

Meanwhile, the mechanic was looking for a boat, an anchor, and the chain, which normally go together. However, he could not see any of them, or the boy's sister. Lachie scolded the lad and warned him that he was a busy man. Lachie told him that he should not lead him to something that did not exist.

Hamish held himself together and promised him, "Honest, sir, it's true. There is an anchor and chain." He didn't mention the creature as he drew near to where he believed the mist was. There was a aloud roar, which by now Hamish had got used to, but Lachie was pale-faced and trying to recover from a boozy night. What he heard wasn't something that he had heard before. He was taken aback by the sound of the roar because he couldn't see anything near him.

Hamish shouted to his sister in the hope she would hear him. "Over here!" his sister responded. Lachie looked and saw nothing. For the first time in his life, he believed his wife and mother-in-law were right: unless he stopped drinking, it would affect his mind.

"Is it too late for that?" Lachie said to himself. He then sat on a rock, refusing to go any farther. He handed the shifter and a small can of WD-40 to Hamish, who could

barely carry them, far less use them. Hamish assured Lachie
that he would not be long and promised he would return
the tool. A confused Lachie wondered from where this roar
came. Where was the boy's sister? What was more confusing
for Lachie was that now Hamish could not be seen either.

It was a clear day with no mist, fog, rain, or drizzle.
Hamish had just disappeared into thin air. When Hamish
got closer to the unseen fog, a window was blown open again
for him to enter. All of this was unknown to Lachie, who by
now was suffering his worst hangover.

Hamish entered the mist, and his sister was overjoyed to
see him. The creature had moved to a position that exposed
the damaged flipper. If Hamish's plan didn't work, the
creature may die. Unknown to the children, the mist had
a life span of only five hours, and already four hours had
passed.

Seonag tried to speak to her brother privately, to tell him
that this creature was the monster of the loch, but Hamish
indicated that he had already figured it out. She told Hamish
that the creature had less than two hours to live unless she
got into the water. By now, Hamish had managed to open
the shifter, which by itself was hard for a small boy. He then
saturated the nut and bolt that kept the shackle on with
the WD-40, trying his hardest not to infect the damaged
skin Getting the shifter around the nut was quite easy, but
making it move was difficult, and there was no way he was
going to get Lachie involved. The secret would have to be
kept. No matter how hard Hamish pulled the shifter, the
nut refused to budge.

"Can you ask Nessie to move the other flipper against the shifter when I give the signal? It may work that way!" Hamish told his sister. Seonag, in her best Gaelic, guided the monster into a position to put pressure on the shifter, to allow the nut to be slackened. The children watched, but nothing happened. Hamish poured more WD-40, and all of a sudden the nut slowly started to unscrew. After several adjustments, the nut was removed!

However, the bolt was still attached. It needed to be shaken so that it would come apart. They started to feel panicky because little time was left. He asked his sister to ask the monster if it was possible to swing the flipper in the air, to see if it would loosen the bolt. As soon as Seonag passed this message on to the monster, they hid behind a boulder for protection.

Meanwhile, Lachie the mechanic was still trying to figure out what was happening. He wanted to leave, but what about his tool? How could he explain about the missing boy? As a Highlander, he wanted to find out everything regarding what was happening. Then all of a sudden, he saw what he believed to be a fighter jet, which usually used the glens for training. The object came closer until it was clear that it was not a fighter jet, but an anchor! Right behind it was a large chain coming through the sky and landing a couple of hundred feet from him. Unable to move, Lachie fell to his knees, for the first time in his life, prayed for sanity. He stayed there for some time, hoping the nightmare would go away.

While Lachie was in this position, Hamish came out

through the mist, pulling the shifter behind him. Hamish thought Lachie may be a religious man, and he did not want to disturb him. He left the shifter beside him and then left because of the time. He quickly ran towards his sister, although he could not see her. He followed her voice until he saw a small, fleshy flap, where his sister was shouting at him to hurry.

Suddenly, they were both in a different world. Their whole lives had completely changed, and no longer were they being motivated by their own senses. They were tossed and turned from side to side. This went on for some time, and eventually it started to calm down little by little.

8

A LL OF A SUDDEN, THEY FELT THAT they were on dry land. They could not figure where they were, and there were no windows to see out of. Then it was as if a light had been switched on – a very powerful light. They felt as though they were not at Loch Ness but in a garden with beautiful flowers surrounding them.

As they admired the beauty around them, they saw in the distance a beautiful woman moving towards them with long silver hair. Although she was old, she still had a young complexion, and as she came closer, she radiated more.

"Don't be afraid. You are now in the palace of my ancestors," she said in English. "I am the last of my family and am expected to carry the family tradition. My desire is to visit the only remaining dinosaur, with me entangled with the anchor and chain for eight years, it was impossible for me to attempt the journey. Now that I'm free, I hope to accomplish my desires. All I wanted was to bring the golden egg back to Loch Ness, so it would be hatched here to preserve the heritage of the dinosaurs. This is the first time in eight years that I am pain-free, thanks to you two. I have never spoken to humans before. My dream proved right. Young lady, you mentioned Odessa."

She then asked Seonag to show her the newspaper cuttings, regarding where they were heading. Seonag produced the crumpled piece of paper, tried to make it straight, and handed it to her. As Nessie read in silence, she dropped the paper and excused herself to her parlour.

Is she upset with something? Seonag thought.

The children admired their surroundings and wondered whether this could be the heaven that Grandma had spoken about. "There are no monsters in heaven!" blurted Seonag. This was according to Grandma, and her word was gospel.

After some time, Nessie returned to them with a smile on her face. She made herself comfortable and introduced herself not as Nessie the monster, but as Maggie. Maggie paused for a moment and looked them in the eye. Tears fell down her face like a child. She said, "I have something to tell you, but before I do, I want to show you a screen."

In a flash, a beautiful screen appeared. It wasn't like a normal television. It was so clear and showed a map. Maggie said to them, "I want you to watch the arrow very carefully." As they watched the arrow, she indicated where they needed to go. It showed the orphanage of dreams, which was in Odessa.

"Listen carefully. This is where my friend lives, only seven miles from the orphanage of dreams. Such a coincidence!"

Hamish looked at Seonag with excitement. Maggie changed the tone of her voice and told the children, "You're my responsibility while you're here. Should you need to return to Loch Ness, that can happen in an instance, and you will not remember being here."

The children looked at each other for a moment, and then they answered together that they wanted to stay with her. Maggie smiled without answering their wishes.

"What if I had left you on the lakeside once I got free from the anchor and chain? It would have been much easier for me to have left you on the shores on Loch Ness. But a word appeared on my internal screen that I couldn't understand: selfish. I thought I knew all the fish in the sea except this one. It was revealed to me on the screen what it actually means. And now you are here. I felt it was my duty to you both, and to my ancestors, to fulfil one more mission with many dangers. You wanting to stay with me indicates that you wish to accompany me on this mission."

Hamish and Seonag smiled.

Maggie continued. "My choice will be your choice. But the mission is possible. You simply need to adjust to the plan I have put in place. I truly believe that we can make it. Whether I make it back, I cannot say. At the palace, there are no clocks; time does not exist A room has been arranged for you both so you can sleep."

The children could not believe what was going on, and they forgot about the mechanic and their parents. Smelling food for the first time that day was something special. Bowls filled with food were brought in, but they looked different. "You have to eat it all up!" commanded Maggie. She meant it literally – the bowls as well as the contents. They had never tasted anything as great as this.

Maggie was confused when she saw them close their eyes and utter something as if they were talking to someone. When Hamish and Seonag finished praying, Maggie asked to whom they were speaking. "Is it a tribal issue?" quizzed Maggie.

Hamish shook his head. "We were giving thanks to God for the food," he explained. "It's a prayer Grandma taught us when she was alive. We've been doing it ever since we can remember."

Maggie smiled. She did not interrogate them any further, although it was something new for her to consider. *But it was I who gave then the food,* Maggie said to herself.

The children were led to a smaller parlour with feathery beds, and within minutes of sinking into the beds, they were asleep. After an uncomfortable sleep on the hard, grassy shore the night before, they greatly enjoyed the bed of feathers.

Maggie watched over them for a time and reflected upon what she had done for the first time in hundreds of years. No human had known the heart of Nessie. She wasn't totally aware of the state of her monster outer skin and the pain she would go through. Although she was clear from the anchor and chain, she would feel pain until her flipper healed. She was Nessie to the world, but to the dinosaur world she was

Maggie. She had no idea of time, but she knew that the adventure would start very soon.

Back at the loch side, Lachie eventually got off his knees. The first thing he noticed was the shifter sitting next to him, but there was no Hamish. Lachie picked up the shifter and headed towards his van. He glanced back, but all he could see was a normal lochside, with tourists mingling about. He could hear the laughter of children, and everything seemed as it had been for years.

For Lachie, there was a missing link. Like many people from the Western Isles, it was not unusual to speak to oneself, but this time Lachie was stuck for words. He threw the shifter into the back of his vehicle and drove back to the garage. He had told so many stories in his life to his boss, to cover up his days of drinking. Why should his boss believe him today when he told the

truth? He pulled into the garage, expecting to be interrogated.

The day went on as usual, and his withdrawal from alcohol had subsided. It was Saturday, and all the people in the garage went home early. That evening Lachie was in no hurry to leave. It was also payday, and normally it would be a run from the garage to the bar. Not today – he had enough in his head without filling his brain with whisky. He tried to put this into perspective and think about what alcohol had done to his mind. He was reliving the memory of the afternoon. There was something missing; it was not coming together.

How did the boy disappear? How could I not see the sister who yelled? Where did the roar come from, and how did the shifter come back? Lachie thought. There were so many questions that he wanted answered. As Lachie sat in a small recliner in the garage to ponder on the stability of his mental health, he thought back to his parents, who were good living people. He himself was a good man and willing to help anybody, but he realised he was known for his binge drinking, and people laughed at him. He accepted it because it was easier that way.

Lachie decided to make amends to his crooked ways and do something he had not done for a long time: he would pass the bar and go straight home from his work. He brought the van back to the workshop and remembered that the shifter was still in the back. When he picked it up and laid it beside his own tools, he noticed something strange. The shifter was still open, and between the jaws was a nut that looked as though it had been rounded by force. The jaws of the shifter looked melted. He put the shifter into a vice and hammered at the nut until it came free. The nut was rounded as if it had been in a furnace. He locked up and headed home.

Lachie took off his shoes at the door, as he did whether drunk or sober. He took a shower, got dressed, and had supper. This was quite normal, but Lachie always came home drunk. For his wife, Morag, it was hard to converse with a man who was always drunk on a Saturday, as well as six of the other nights of the week, so she wasn't prepared to make any conversation. But something was odd tonight. He was too good, and some wives would have a problem with that, so poor Lachie was in a no-win situation.

He was up early on the Sunday and got dressed in his

best clothes. Now Morag was up to high doh. "Where is he going dressed up?" wondered Morag.

"I am off to church." Of course, there was nothing wrong with going to church!

But the reason that led him to go to church was unknown to his wife of twenty-five years.

Lachie was a watched man by his neighbours in the community, and more so by his wife. Lachie's new lifestyle was totally out of character to anything he had ever done before. People found it hard to believe that he could keep this up. They believed it wasn't a change of spiritual heart, but that he was simply trying to wind them up. However, time went on, and Lachie continued to go to church. People would not take the seat where he normally sat at the bar, because they thought if they did, Lachie would grab them and throw them off. Now there was no Lachie, but for some reason they gave him respect and would not sit on his seat.

One Saturday afternoon, out of curiosity he decided to venture again to the shores of Loch Ness to get some satisfaction and get some answers surrounding this mystical anchor and chain, which kept coming back to his mind. He drove to the place where he believed Hamish and himself left the van. Lachie knew all the boulders and stones, and even the outline of the loch, which made it quite easy to return to the location. As he got closer, everything looked in order, and there was nothing out of the ordinary. He then decided to give up and head home.

All of a sudden, he saw a seagull perched on the bent, rusty anchor. He walked towards it and ran into a chain. He stopped to examine the chain and noticed the last link had a shackle hanging with a bent bolt, as if it were ripped apart by a great force. Lachie bent down and took the nut from his pocket. To his horror, it matched the bolt.

He paused for a moment. *There is something greater than just the deterioration of my mental health,* he thought. Even if he told this to people, they would not believe him. "What really happened that day?" they'd ask. After walking away from the chain, he decided to put the issue out of his mind, which was not an easy task. Loch Ness had kept her secrets for a long time. Could Lachie keep this story a secret forever? He knew that if he drank again, the whole thing would come out.

One Sunday as Lachie was doing his usual trip to church, he was getting ready to drive home. A couple whom he'd known a long time stopped by and rolled down a car window to speak to him. "How are you doing, Lachie?" they asked.

"Fine. How are you doing?" he answered.

The woman turned to Lachie and said, "There's something I want to ask you."

"Go ahead, my dear."

There was a pause in the conversation. "A few weeks ago, we gave a young boy a lift to the garage. He was a nice boy, although he probably would have been nicer if he had just told the truth."

By this time, Lachie wanted to hear every word she was saying. He had forgotten everything that the minister had said. "What was his story?" Lachie asked.

"He said he was coming to look for a shifter and WD-40,

and that there was a chain and anchor wrapped round a monster's flipper. he added that his sister was looking after the monster, while he came to the garage," the woman continued. Lachie stared at the woman, and she paused and asked, "Are you okay, Lachie?"

Lachie was stuck for words, and he couldn't answer the woman. He indicated that he needed to go home for lunch.

After driving his way home, he stared at the steering wheel and thought to himself that this whole thing was growing legs – and for some reason, it was making sense. *Did this really happen? Maybe my sanity is okay. Maybe it wasn't the drink after all.*

In that moment, a thought went through Lachie's head. *So I can drink again.*

At home, he sat down to have Sunday lunch. He picked at it, eating a bit of meat and a little bit of vegetables, but Lachie had lost his appetite.

As Morag was watching him, she wondered, *Does he have another woman in his life? Or maybe he has done something so terrible that he can't even eat his dinner.*

9

THE CHILDREN TOSSED AND TURNED in their beautiful bed, and eventually they woke, even though there was no way of measuring time. They looked around at their beautiful surroundings.

Although they'd spent many summer nights in Grandma's house, this morning was different. As they looked around everywhere, it seemed as though all the furniture was built within the structure of the walls.

"How long did we sleep?" the children wondered. They remembered Maggie saying that time was no part of her life; yesterday was gone, and so was the past. They had no clock, no calendar, no Monday to Sunday. Maggie lived in a place that had no time, no yesterday, and only today. In Maggie's world, they were living the dream. The reality was that they were in a beautiful feathered bed and had no idea how long they had slept.

The mattress felt so light that they thought they were floating on air, and the room temperature was just right. There were no clothes all over the place; everything was in order. Despite having no sunshine, the room was full of light, with no dullness in any part. Every corner had an air of excitement The beautiful carpet, which looked as though it had grown there. It felt soft and thick like a flower bed.

They were gleaning on the spoils of joy, and for the first time in their lives, they felt wanted. They felt as though somebody cared, and this was a big thing to them. They had thought they would have to wait until they got to the orphanage of dreams to feel peace.

Maggie appeared right in front of their eyes from nowhere, looking radiant. As she came closer, it made the children feel more relaxed and comfortable.

"Did you sleep well?" she asked.

"Yes, we did!" they answered in chorus.

"That's great to hear. Well, your breakfast is ready, and when you're done, there is something I need to show you. When you have eaten and washed up, I will take you to my parlour. You'll be the first human to enter. In fact, very few of my own ancestors were ever allowed in the parlour. When my family lived in this area, it was out of bounds to most of them. But you are different – you saved my life. However, when you leave here, you will remember nothing about the palace."

After breakfast, they were led into what looked like a beautiful beach, with water so clear that no soap was needed. The heat dried their skin, and all around them it smelled of beautiful flowers. The water changed colours, as did the light; all the colours of the rainbow seemed to come across the water. It was a moment of tranquillity for them, and never could they imagine such a washroom could be so large and beautiful. They were left there to enjoy it for some time.

After their peaceful wash, they were summoned to Maggie's parlour, the main part of the palace. They followed her to a stairway, which led up a level. As they got to the last step, the first thing that they came to were two large granite pillars that were sparkling as if the sun shined off them. As they gazed at all the beautiful lights, they noticed there were no power points, no switches. It was so different from anything they had ever seen. If they had grown to be one hundred years old, they doubt would not have experienced anything else that came close to this. The ornaments all around looked old, as if they were built into the parlour.

The children were summoned to sit down on a seat that did not look like a sofa or couch, but they sank down until they reached a great comfort.

The children were given time to settle. It was a place where no human had ever been. When stillness came, there was a sense of peace and serenity. It was a scene that everybody in the world wanted: no worries, no time, one's blood pressure perfect, no bills, no discomfort, no turning the TV from channel to channel, no rustling of papers, no sounds of phones or the doorbell. At last they were in a place to which only dreams could bring them.

They felt a little sadness for the many children who would

sit at the loch side and had waited through many hours of travel, just to get a glimpse of Nessie.

"You are in a place of beauty. It's my paradise, and everything here is perfect. However, we will be on the human timescale once we leave this habitation. We will be open to the elements of your world and what it throws at us. This habitation, which goes back many centuries, is mine; no man can claim it today, tomorrow, or any day. It is protected in a way you would not understand.

"As I explained earlier, a golden egg is required from the last remaining dinosaur monster, which I believe is still alive. I've decided to bring you with me, but should things go wrong in a split second, you will find yourself on the shores of Loch Ness again. You will remember nothing about your experience with me."

Maggie continued with a smile. "I am telling you the negative parts to prepare you, but very soon we will set off. We are now coming to the part of the briefing that may be a bit uncomfortable for you. It will almost be impossible for you to travel with me in deep water, or saltwater. You would not survive in the conditions we are about to experience. We are sitting here in this beautiful parlour, but it's different out there."

The children had no idea what was coming next. Never in their wildest dreams could they imagine what Maggie was about to utter to them. She smiled and said, "Don't be afraid – it's all part of the plan for your survival throughout the journey."

She then looked at the children with a serious face. She

told them that in order to enable them to survive the journey, they would have to be changed from children to dinosaurs in the human dimension. She would call two of her ancestors from the grave, and that was what they would be changed into.

"Hamish you will be thirty-eight years old, and your name will be Archie, after my great-great granddad. He was a prince in the land of the ancestors – a very good-looking, strong, and fearless young man. You will have the responsibility to help and care for the wounded flipper, be in charge of navigation, and help with the route that is already prepared."

Seonag was taken aback that her brother was going to be a prince. As she looked at him, he grinned from ear to ear, beat his chest, and threw back his curly ginger hair.

Maggie noticed that Seonag was a bit downcast. She thought it was funny how humans reacted to someone else getting something. Maggie's eyes fell on Seonag as if she felt sorry for the way she reacted. She said, "Your name will be changed to Betty, and you will be thirty-nine years old. Betty was well-known many years ago. She was known for her compassion, but what made her so well-known was her ability to battle equally with any male. She was very beautiful – in fact, she was more beautiful than any human woman."

Maggie showed Seonag a picture of her, and she pointed to what did not look like a picture until Seonag focused her eyes on it; then it showed the beauty of the woman.

The children had gone from nobody's child to a prince and Princess, which brought great excitement to them.

For many years, they had been through a lot together and carried a lot of each other's burdens when times were hard. They knew they weren't like normal children, but they made the best of life. There were times when all they had were each other. This new experience was a long way from sitting at the riverside in Cruach na Moine.

As the children settled down, they forgot that this change still hadn't taken place. Would they die and then come back? They had no idea what was about to happen to them, and soon they would be someone else who was a thousand years old but also had a human age. Their minds had no capacity to understand this. After they were left alone, tears ran down Seonag's face. She hugged her brother and said, "Remember that time you were blamed for stealing from the cookie jar, and you were sent to bed? Well, it was I who stole them, not you. I'm sorry."

Hamish would have scolded her under normal circumstances, but these were not normal circumstances. He went quiet for a moment, and then he reminded Seonag of the time the middle part of her favourite book was missing. She straightened her back with a shock. She was sure it was not her brother who'd taken it, because he helped her to look for the missing parts. She then smiled and said, "You bad boy. I forgive you." The children both stood there saying sorry to each other as if they were never going to see each other again.

The moment to change came, and they were no longer

Seonag and Hamish. Maggie was confronted by her ancestors Betty and Archie. Archie was unshaven, had a few missing teeth and curly greying hair and was very red-faced as if he had been outside a lot. Betty looked better and had a good complexion. Archie asked when they were going to leave, because they were still on a human timescale. They were aware of the journey but had limited information given to them. The more they went on, the more it would be fed to them. Both Betty and Archie would now be briefed about the journey.

10

WHAT HAPPENED ON LOCH NESS with the anchor and chain should not have happened. As Nessie got older, things were not as they were when she'd been young.

Nessie made signs to Archie and Betty that they were ready to leave the palace. In an instant they were within the outer body of Nessie, and the first thing they noticed was the human temperature, along with the pain which came from the damaged flipper. As Nessie was about to leave the palace, she spoke a code in order to secure he palace.

They were in the outer skin which was now Nessie, and all of a sudden with one motion, they were off from the place she loved so much. As they swung away from the habitation, within seconds Nessie was in the middle of the loch.

She wanted to circle the loch before they left for two reasons: to say goodbye to her homeland, and to see that all was well with the flipper and the rest of her body, which would be getting buffeted from the oceans. Her first part of the journey would be precarious, going through a fourteen-mile tunnel to Loch Morar and then a short tunnel to the open sea.

She would soon submerge to a great depth to get parallel with the tunnel between the two lochs. The tunnel was very narrow and had many twists and turns. There were many other tunnels that led from the main one.

From his monitors, Archie could see the flipper that was damaged was causing discomfort to his leader. Betty surveyed the blood system, which looked reasonable. They had only just set off, and so it would take time for everything to settle down. The night-vision eyes were essential for Nessie not only in the dark but also to help in the deep tunnel under the lochs between Loch Ness and Loch Morar.

Nessie dropped slowly with no sound from the crew on board, which was watching the monitors. They kept dropping and slowly began to move in a direction that the built-in compass showed. Nessie sped up, and when she was a quarter of a mile from the entrance of the tunnel, she began to think that the entrance may be tighter. No one had entered for several years, since Nessie had made her last journey. The tunnel was not straight – far from it. She had to make sure not to take a wrong turn. In order to combat this, Nessie had instruments available for navigation purposes, but it was her instincts that gave her the best results and were her greatest asset. She entered the tunnel. Tunnels were always dark, even on the surface. Once she started, there was no going back. Next stop: Morar.

All of a sudden, she felt a huge thud on her back. Nessie had touched a corner, which almost turned her completely over and put her on an uneven keel. Her crew were shaken, and Archie used words that humans would be proud of. She slowed down for a while as the damaged flipper caused problems. Manoeuvring in the tunnel was quite hard due to no light and no space to move. The journey was becoming bumpier because of the lack of speed. One of the monitors that Archie and Betty watched was to calculate the distance and time that remained to the end of the tunnel.

There was only a certain time that Nessie could stay underwater, and any hold-ups would be a concern. Nessie was made aware that they'd come up against a wall. She managed to figure out that part of the tunnel had caved in, and she couldn't go back. This was a situation that she dreaded – to be stuck in a tunnel underwater with no escape route. Time was running out, and this was a cause for alarm. She told the crew to hold tight as she pushed forward with all her strength, but nothing happened. For a moment, she thought of something. The children Seonag and Hamish had prayed before they ate, and they kept looking up towards the sky, noting their Bible stories about Jesus saving the world. She thought, *This is the moment Nessie needs saving.* Well, if it was good enough for Grandma, it was good enough for Nessie.

Nessie was still stuck, and she couldn't go forward or backward, which made the situation precarious. She decided to look up with her night eyes and focus. After few minutes, she saw the hole that had fallen on her, and she thought that if she attempted to go up instead of forward, things might be different. She cleared all debris round her. With her air time running down to thirty-two minutes, she decided to get into a position. She hoped this would not disturb any more of the tunnel and allow her to use the night glasses to see any clearances that would be able to get her to the other side of the blockage.

Nessie started to rise up and go back down again, but there was still a lot of debris. She shook her large body, and much of it fell off, but there was a danger that the debris from her back would jam her in. She began to push backward and forward to loosen herself. She tried a second time and felt looser, and this time she managed to rise above the area that was trapping her.

She could see beyond the blockage to the collapsed tunnel. There was a fair distance ahead that she could travel. This seemed to be a lifeline, and she hoped it would continue. Once again, it was the children who seemed to have saved her life, or someone they knew very well.

She went farther through the tunnel. Eventually, to her great delight she found herself in the original tunnel. Now she had to speed up to get to the end of the tunnel and make it to the surface of Loch Morar.

As they started to come to the surface, it was still very dark because her night glasses and her whole body were covered in mud. She came to the surface and allowed oxygen to be taken on board and to chill out for a moment.

It was the middle of the night, and there was very little chance of anybody being on the loch. She surfaced, and all of a sudden, an internal warning light came on indicating that they were in the vicinity of humans. Very soon she would have to make an emergency dive. After a few moments, Nessie decided to submerge and head for the last tunnel, which was only half a mile long.

The tunnel was used many times by otters, salmon, and eels and shouldn't have any problems. Soon they were out the other side, where she had to adapt to saltwater.

With the moon, up she could see the islands of Rum, Eigg, and Muck. By breakfast she would be getting close to the Irish Sea.

Archie examined the damaged flipper and gave Nessie a report. He told her that it looked gruesome, but he believed it was repairable. Nessie kept her thoughts to herself and knew that the situation in the tunnel was too close for comfort. The next part of the journey should be easier.

They were making good time – back on even keel, as they say! Life was strange: one minute they had all these problems, and then all of a sudden things were good again. However, as they kept swimming and making their way towards the Irish Sea, they were not aware that they had been spotted on Loch Morar by humans.

On the shores of Loch Morar, three poachers who came across the monster in the middle of the night were terrified. The sighting had lasted for only a few seconds, but it was enough to make the poachers head for dry land. They would leave the loch this night without any salmon. They huddled together all night in an old Bothy, going over the experience. They couldn't put it to sleep and forget all about what had happened. The world had to know what had happened on Loch Morar that night. They had to approach the story from a different angle. The place for stories was the bar. Stories were built and destroyed in bars. Small fish catches were made bigger, and many romance stories were taken well out of context. The Morar bar was no different.

11

THE POACHERS' ORDEAL HAPPENED AT night, so their story couldn't be told until the opening of the bar, which was eleven in the morning. They calmly strolled into the bar as they usually would.

These poachers will not be given any names in case of legal matters, and this book is not based on the whole truth but is close to it. As they talked amongst themselves, the bartender noticed their conversation was very secret, which only happened when they were in trouble. One of the poachers started to cry as if someone had spilt his drink. "He had a bad experience on Loch Morar," one of his colleagues said.

But as far as the bartender could see, there were no signs of any injury. He asked if they were with him during the time of the bad experience, and there was silence.

Someone else asked, "Did you see a ghost?" The highlands

of Scotland were renowned for ghost stories. Some sounded real, and some were obvious lies. However, these men could not keep it to themselves for long, especially in a bar where there was alcohol.

Across the bar and listening in was a retired journalist. Although retired, he thought he could make a few quid by calling his old colleagues who still worked for the press. He asked the bartender to give the three poachers three large ones. In the Scottish highlands, this was three large whiskies, which was a measure that would allow them to taste what they were drinking.

All eyes were on these poachers, believing that something out of the ordinary was going on. People wanted to find out why the poachers were acting so curiously. The crying poacher started waving around his small 127 Brownie camera, which he used to take pictures of his catch of salmon, but he would always make sure he did not allow the picture to give away where they were caught.

"The evidence is in here!" he said while waving his camera. He repeated it over and over again.

By this time, the journalist took a seat much closer. He thought that someone had a scoop.

Just then, the bar door sprung open, and in came a well-dressed, middle-aged man who was not in the best of humour. The man made a beeline to the three poachers, pointing his finger and shouting, "You took my boat again, after promising you would not take it! But you did, and you left an oar sticking out. It's been chewed up by a couple of cows. Now the oar is knackered!"

The sobbing poacher stood up and told the owner that he had taken the boat. This came as a surprise to the other poachers. "It wasn't a cow that chewed the oar, but a monster! It was the monster that attacked me last night! If we had told you guys this morning, you would not believe us. As I fought the monster, it turned away from me. I managed to take a picture on this camera. Whether it will come out when the film is developed is a different story."

The journalist was now at the table, having pulled his chair over. He tried to make a call to one of his buddies.

The bar was full because everyone wanted to hear about the fight on Loch Morar. This sort of story would bring people from near and far to the cash-strapped area. A monster on Loch Morar was good for publicity.

The two young men who went to get the film developed soon returned with the developed film. With excitement the sobbing man fumbled through the pictures. He found some pictures of large salmon, some of his colleagues, and then two that looked blank.

When he came to the last picture in the pack, he had a big grin on this face. The crowd quietened and gathered round. The picture had been taken at 2:0 a.m. and had a very dark background, but right in the middle they could see very vividly an unusual creature. They could not see the whites of its eyes, but there was enough to satisfy the gathering that this was a real story. This photographic evidence gave the story an element of truth, which went a long way to help the poacher. The picture was priceless.

As they spoke, a man with a large camera on his back

came into the bar, followed by men with notebooks. The private press conference the men had between themselves was no longer private. Not only the locals of Morar would hear about this, but the whole of the country and far beyond.

Nevertheless, there was a missing link, and somehow things didn't quite add up. Fighting a monster with one hand while holding a camera and an oar in the other hand was a mystery. This would not be settled tonight or tomorrow. One thing was for sure: these men would not be on the loch tonight. They would be getting their pictures taken beside the boat and the chewed oar. What a scoop for the press!

The next morning, there was mayhem in the village. It was overrun by press from all over the world, searching for a glimpse of the hero who'd fought the monster. Although not everyone was happy, the other two poachers were not getting the same publicity as their pal. At one point during the day, they pulled him aside by reminding him that he had not fought any monster, and that it was a cow that had chewed the oar. They added that they were in this together.

After his friends finished, the old poacher burst out laughing in their faces and replied, "Who's crying now?" He took no notice of them. It was in times like this that good friends had a falling out, and the two jealous poachers would make sure he tripped himself up.

The next day, there was only one hero in all the papers. Was it a monster who chewed the oar, or was it a cow? In the *Washington Free Post*, it was monster. In the *Japanese Herald*, it was a monster. In the *West Highland Free Hong Kong* press, it was a monster. That was all the world wanted to hear, and monster mania spread like wildfire. From that day on, the three poachers weren't friends and only spoke to each other in church.

12

THE LIGHTS OF OIL RIGS MADE THE SEA less boring. When they looked out to sea, normally all they could see were waves all around. Nessie was going to have to board an oil rig. This boarding would be onto a semi-submergible, and she would land on the spider deck, which was up from the sea and was normally between the four legs of an oil rig.

When the weather was severe and rough, the waves covered the spider deck. That was why very little was stored there This was where Nessie intended to land in order to carry out some emergency repair on the damaged flipper. Going back to Loch Ness was not an option.

Nessie was still a distance away from the intended rig, but the timing had to be right, and it had to be done when the oil men went to lunch. On the night shift, darkness provided part of the cover, but on the oil rig she would use her camouflage mist.

The landing would be precarious and dangerous for all concerned. At the moment, all that was on Nessie's mind was fulfilling the dreams of the two children, as well as hoping to see her beloved friend, Uisdean.

This operation would have to be completed within one hour and ten minutes, which was the length of the night shift oil men's lunch break. This window left no room for error, and as always there would be things that were not straightforward. They were now within a mile and a half of the oil rig, called the Bent Bravo. They had a mind picture of the spider deck, which was fairly large and open to the four winds.

The weather was strong, and this would be in Nessie's favour because the strong winds and wave surge would help the landing. Nessie would time her boarding on the spider deck when the sea waves came close enough to the deck.

Betty and Archie were informed that they were within half a mile of the rig. Nessie submerged just below the surface of the waves and informed them that she was parallel with the leg of the rig. Nessie was now using her dynamic positioning ability and awaiting a large wave that would help the landing.

She began to surface, and as a twelve-meter wave broke, she sprang into action on the crest of the large wave. Seven seconds was a long time on the crest of a wave. With Nessie's own strength, she leaped and lunged onto the spider deck. In a split second, the camouflage mist, which Nessie used to hide herself from the outside world, was in place. Within seconds, Betty and Archie were released on deck.

As soon as his feet hit the spider deck, Archie made his way up a windy staircase, where he found three boxes of ceramic fibre wool. They'd use it to support and protect the wound.

The flipper lay motionless as Betty made her way to inspect it. She detected a strong smell coming from the wound. This was not good news, and as she got closer, she could see parts were infected, which made it impossible to stitch. She got Archie for a second opinion. He looked at the wound, and within a minute he was off again. Back up the winding stairway, he found a six-inch grinder and extension cable. Betty watched him with her mouth and eyes wide open, wondering what was going on in his head. Betty could not believe that he was going to use this to tear away the infected area.

The six-inch grinder was usually used for rig decks and for grinding steel plates or pipes. They examined the area that needed to be cut off; it was the only way that this wound could be stitched, because stitches would not hold unless it was inserted into healthy flesh. This part of the operation was using a great deal of precious time – they had already lost thirty minutes.

Archie told Betty, "Stand clear." He expected a grave reaction once he started to cut into a nerve. Getting on anybody's nerve was one thing but getting on Nessie's nerve was something else. Archie focused on the area that needed to be cut, and for him this was a first.

The outer dead skin was quite easy to remove, but as Archie went beyond the dead skin, Nessie let out a scream, and her body moved almost to the other side of the spider deck, throwing Betty and Archie sprawling across the deck. After they gathered themselves together, Archie attempted to carry on.

When they were satisfied that it was clear of any dead skin, sewing the wound would not be easy. The swelling made it much harder than expected. Knitting it into the skin would be painful, but this was the only way to stop the bleeding. Archie started to stitch with an old roll of rusty wire. This was not in line with the NHS Health Board procedures, but they both worked together, and the wound started to close. Archie unrolled the fibre wool round the flipper, using all three boxes that they had available in order to protect the wound. Wire on the outer side was required to tighten the fibre, followed by fire blanket to protect the fibre wool

Seven minutes were left of the allocated time. At this point Archie, Betty, and even Nessie were not aware that the jump from Nessie at the start of the cutting of the skin had set off the rig alarms from the control room on the rig. When those alarms went off, all the oil men must go to a muster point with life jackets.

13

BETTY AND ARCHIE WERE SAFELY ON
board Nessie, and it was a time to allow the fog to lift
so that Nessie could make her entrance into the water. This
time she could not afford to wait for a big wave. The only
thought on her mind was to lift off and get back into the
water. She would still not be able to use the damaged flipper,
so she depended on the power of her two back flippers.

The take-off failed the first time. With her second
attempt, she cleared the rig – but only after she had hurled
herself against one of the legs of the rig, shaking it more than
damaging it. The thud was heard by all the oil men, who
were already tired and frustrated.

Were the men who were mustered in serious danger? Was
it sabotage? They looked at all issues. One of the operators
in the control room, who was in charge of monitoring the
CCTV, paused for a moment while looking at a camera. He

rewound the camera and could not believe what he saw. He called over several of his companions to look at his monitor.

There was only nine seconds of tape that showed what looked like a monster lunging from the spider deck and then bouncing off one of the legs. As they looked at each other, these burly oil men became speechless. How would they make an announcement to the oil men who had been mustered? The manager knew he could not stand them down without an answer.

The offshore insulation manager, or OIM, was keyed up for moments of danger and trained to make decisions and explanations, but this time it was different. He eventually made a statement for the men to stand down and come to the cinema after a smoke break, hot drink, and some cookies. Confused and irritated, the men were in no mood, and they felt that those in high positions were hiding something from them.

They were there before the scheduled time, sitting and waiting. The OIM had managed to get his team to transfer the CCTV onto the cinema screen. The tired men settled in their seats, ready to get some answers. The wildest oil men did not expect what they were about to see.

When the OIM entered the cinema, he was given respect, and all focus was on his forthcoming statement. It was seldom that these men in high positions struggled to stay in control.

"I am about to show you nine seconds of film," he said, and the lights dimmed. At first it was just a view of the spider deck, but as the men stared at the screen, all of a sudden a monster appeared for nine long seconds.

One oil man shouted that it was his mother-in-law. The rest were speechless. This changed the attitude of the men from anger to excitement, even though they were tired. They were told that the majority of them would be sent home at first light as a precautionary measure.

The news travelled fast. The oil men called home, only to be told by their wives that they should sober up. Many of the wives queried whether they were on an oil rig or at a night club. "Monster my foot," was the average reply from the agitated loved ones. "I'll monster him when he gets home," murmured one wife.

However, they would read the papers that evening, and the astonishing news was worldwide. Was there a Loch Morar connection? Of course there was – if the papers said it, then it was true.

The flipper that had been repaired was holding well, with no blood being lost. Nessie was making good speed and was now in open water, well away from the rig. She and her crew were now heading towards the Spanish coast.

Nessie knew that the few seconds between the clearing of her mist on the spider deck and her getting into the water could have caused a problem. Betty and Archie were having a well-deserved rest, and at present it was best for them to stay out of Nessie's way because they had inflicted much pain on their boss. Betty and Archie were part of Nessie: when Nessie ate, they also ate; when Nessie drank, they drank when Nessie, yes they did.

The world believed there was a connection between Loch Morar and the oil rig incident. Was there a monster roaming the ocean? Throughout the world, monster mania made it difficult for children to study, and people at work stood around, discussing the monster instead of working. TV news was breaking all records. This was fresh to the world. Where was the loose cannon going to strike next? Forget sports – the word *monster* was on everybody's lips.

14

THE WARM WEATHER MADE IT MORE bearable for Nessie to swim through the strong tides of the Spanish shores. She swam mostly below the surface of the ocean; this was the way she had lived for many years in Loch Ness. If the tourists came to look for her over the summer and winter, spotting her every day, the excitement would wear off. The mystery remained and speculation of her existence went on.

She hoped to make a stop to check her wounded flipper before she continued her journey. Cyprus was the place she planned to stop. While ashore in Cyprus, it would be the right time to bring Hamish and Seonag back for a period of time. She felt the children needed a period of time out in the fresh air.

The last part of the journey would be the most precarious. It would be dangerous at the secret naval base, which would be protected in a certain way so that if anything came within a certain radius, it would be detected. If they believed they were in danger of the high-tech submarine basin being discovered, they would press an emergency button that would blow up the base, and there would be no trace of evidence to be found. This was Nessie's trump card, and hopefully this would allow her within the lake to continue unfinished business. There was no way round getting into the lake where Uisdean hopefully lived. Also, the orphanage of dreams was only a few miles away. This part of the journey would be dangerous. Fighting against an army had to be done with a mind game.

Nessie approached the fishing ground as the sun started to set. She could make out two boats, which seemed quite a distance apart. Many fishing boats worked in pairs, which was called pair trawling. Two boats had a large net between them, and they lowered the net by wires to the required depth, pulling the net towards where the fish were. There was a danger that Nessie could get caught between the two boats and end up in the net, which would be a disaster for Nessie and the two fishing boats.

Nessie decided to submerge and hoped to swim under the net. The water in this area was quite deep. After swimming for some time, she believed she was out of danger from the net.

Just then, Archie indicated that for some reason, his equipment showed that she was slowing down. "Is there something wrong?" Archie called out.

Nessie glanced at her panel. To her horror, she saw herself

being dragged backwards and deep into the net. She had to outwit the two boats with her speed and strength; otherwise, she would find herself caught up by the net and amongst the caught fish. Unless she got free this could possibly end her secret life!

The two boats, *Tudor Rose* and *Prosperity*, realised that something was seriously wrong. Duncan and Sandy were highly experienced skippers, and there were times they would pick up large stones in the net that became quite a problem. However, this time it seemed to be something much bigger. As the two skippers struggled to pull in the long wires on their winches, the winches began to smoke because of the weight.

It was frightening to see two boats being pulled backward and in a position they couldn't control. Eventually a decision had to be made about whether to let the wires go and completely lose all the fishing equipment. At least it would save their boats and the lives of their crew. These skippers put the lives of the men before the equipment.

Meanwhile, Nessie had a plan that may work. It would put the life of Archie in danger.

At the end of the net was a cod end with a latch. This part of the net would normally be pulled onto the fishing boat and would release the fish onto the deck. The plan was to release Archie from herself. He would then cut a hole in the net to make his way down the outside of the net and release the latch, which would allow the fish – but more important, Nessie – to get a second chance and be free once again.

Archie had only a knife but was ready. The two boats

were in danger of being pulled underwater. This operation was one that had to work. As Archie was released, he made his exit through one of Nessie's gills and into the net. He hung onto the net with fish around him. He found it was very hard with one hand on the net and the other keeping the fish from his face. He held the knife in his mouth. Once he had overcome the disorientation, he was able to cut the very strong marshes in the net, which were fairly large.

Once outside, he could see clearer that he was quite a distance from the cod end. He made his way down slowly, inch by inch. The whole operation depended on him; if he failed, they all failed. He continued to crawl and got struck with several jellyfish, which had a powerful sting.

Nessie was trying to swim within the net until Archie released the latch; then all would be well. But things didn't usually go according to plan, and this was no different. Archie crawled and struggled to hold on. He knew how important this was to all concerned.

He was only two feet from the latch and could see the large rope attached to the cod end. Archie used the rope to guide him to the latch. At last he was close to the latch, which was made of hard steel and fixed with a wedge insert. It looked easy to release, but the weight of fish against it made it almost impossible. Archie used the rope attached to the latch to coil around his hand. This would give him more purchase to pull the latch, and hopefully he could release the fish and poor Nessie. Archie struggled to the point that was near a point of despair, but giving up was not an option.

He had to find a way because he knew Nessie would be

watching him. As the rope dangled before him, he thought of a plan that seemed to be a long shot. He followed the long rope that was tied to the cod end, dislodged it, fastened it to the latch, and brought the other end to Nessie. Was it long enough? He tied it around his waist and made his way back into the net. This was not part of the previous plan, and cutting into the net was just as hard as trying to cut out.

He knew that it was only pride, the fear of Nessie, and the "never say die" lifestyle that kept him going. While struggling to cut his way inside, he managed to cut enough and get in. Once inside, Nessie wasn't hard to find. In fact, as he got inside, she was staring at him, her big blue eyes looking blurred by the motion of the net. She knew his plan and his decision to bring the rope was the right decision. Little did he know that it was Nessie who'd planned this manoeuvre.

Archie was now inside and close to Nessie. He pulled the rope, which was almost made to measure. What now? He noticed Nessie trying to open her mouth, and as she opened, he saw the white teeth that were like tusks. This was not a time to admire her teeth, and he also knew his job on this task was not done. As he tightened the rope round the larger of the tusks, once it was secured, the mouth started to shut, wedging the rope so it would not slip.

Nessie's mouth was not the place one would want to spend the afternoon, but certainly it was better than fighting with a cod end. Archie was safe enough within her mouth as long as Nessie did not swallow or bring up wind.

Without thought for anything else, Nessie pulled the

rope with her head to one side while jamming Archie with her tongue, to prevent him from getting hurt. As Nessie. Pulled her head strongly to one side She yelled as if in severe pain. Then something had happened. There was a huge bang, followed by another loud cry of pain that forced Nessie to half open her mouth. This was a scream that no actor could imitate. The latch opened, allowing the release of the fish and a grateful Nessie.

It was as if they were coming over the Niagara Falls. A rush of water gushed out, and the fish were making their way out of the net. Even though the fish made it to the open sea, they had been crushed. Nessie exited the cod end with speed. Another dangerous situation was over, but they were still a long way from Odessa.

15

NESSIE SET COURSE AS IF NOTHING
had happened, but she knew in her heart that once
again she had been sloppy, and this accident could had been
avoided. It wasn't part of her nature to be weak like this.
All her life, she'd made sure that her every step was right.
Perhaps her age was catching up with her. Was this journey
too much for her?

The two boats that were in danger of sinking were released
from whatever was pulling against them. They almost left
the sea, throwing the crew around the deck while pulling in
the wires, which was now quite easy to do. Upon seeing the
net without any fish or anything indicting something was
wrong, they noticed that the cod end was open.

"This is impossible! It could only be opened manually."
The skippers checked the fish plotter, which showed the fish
going into the net, but when they looked closely, they noticed

a figure in the net. They rewound and replayed. Both boats had the same equipment, and the plotters showed the same signal. It looked like a large creature had been swinging around in their net. These two skippers with one hundred years of experience between them were bamboozled.

As they pondered what to do next, they saw a naval ship come alongside. They had asked for assistance when they were in trouble and feared sinking. Naval officers boarded the fishing boats, the crew showed the officers what was on their fishing monitors. They were speechless. How could they report these findings?

Just then, a crew member called Alister called out, "Over here!" everybody looked, and they saw the young man holding a rope. At the end was a large tooth-like tusk. A decision was made to escort both fishing boats to Barcelona until a full investigation could be made. This fishing trip was over. What now for the skippers and crew?

By this time the media were aware something was up. When someone mentioned *monster,* the world media descended on Barcelona. Monster mania swept through the airways yet again. The skippers and the crew were heroes overnight. Was it Nessie? While she was in the net, did she have a fight with a cod, knocking out her tooth?

After several days with the media, their pictures were on all TV channels and newspapers. The fishing boat crews were flown home to a hero's welcome. What was funny that the crew of the *Tudor Rose* came from Mallaig, three miles from Loch Morar, where the poacher had encountered his fight with a monster. Was there room in the Morar bar, when the real brave heroes arrived.

Nessie decided that her next stop would be Cyprus. She reckoned that Portugal would be too dangerous, with many guarding the coastline and watching to see if any monsters were on the beach making sandcastles. She was concerned about the near misses, and she also knew that the most dangerous part of the journey was still to come. She really needed this break before the final push to Odessa.

16

AS THE DUST SETTLED OVER
Barcelona, the Spanish coast started to get back to
normal. Nessie was getting farther away and nearer her short
autumn break. It was many years ago since she'd last visited
the island of Cyprus; it was on her way back from Odessa.

Nessie had one ambition over the last many hundred
years – one that was dangerous and reasonably stupid. She
wanted to walk the sandy beaches no matter where it was,
and do what other people do. The world only knew her in
her outer apparel, Nessie.

She wanted to walk the beach with the two children. To
the outside world, this was pretty normal, but for Nessie,
who spent a lot of her time in her underwater palace, nobody
knew that she had dreams and ambitions, and that there
were times she was lonely.

Surely she could have a dream. The millions who came

to see her probably fantasised many times that she would come face-to-face with them. If she actually did, they would probably run a mile.

The closer she got to Cyprus, the more her body needed a rest. She could see the skyline and the sun starting to disappear in the background. She slowed down and focused on the area and the precautions she had to take. She couldn't afford any more slip-ups. She approached a small gully with a sandy patch below a cliff, which would be ideal for the six-hour stopover. This would be a good rest prior to the final leg of the journey.

Seonag and Hamish were in the land of nod, sleeping since they'd left Scotland. The wonderful power of Nessie had hidden them from all the highs and lows of her adventures. The shadows of the cliffs would help the camouflage during landing. Nessie felt the warm, shallow water, and very soon her flippers would touch the bottom, scratching against the sand. She knew that the landing would wake Archie up, to remove the bandage on the flipper.

As soon as she touched the beach, she released the mist. Although she could see what was going on from the inside, nobody could see her inside the mist. It would be wonderful if this apparatus could be bought on eBay.

Archie made his way from his inner abode and was released into the mist. With his feet on the sand, his job was to inspect the damaged flipper, which had been repaired on the Bent Bravo. To his dismay, all the bandages had been washed away, which was probably caused by hundreds of miles of travel and being caught by the two fishing boats. There were bare stitches that held the huge wound together.

The stitching had been stitched with rusty wire but did the job by keeping the flesh together, but some of the flesh had grown over the wire and caused quite a bit of discomfort for Nessie. Archie screwed up his face while checking the wound, and he turned away. Maybe he was not cut out to be a doctor.

Nessie was quite happy with the flipper. The pain was bearable, and she was about to treat herself to a break outside her outer skin. Archie and Betty had to go into a trance prior to Hamish and Shonag being wakened.

Now was the opportunity to bring the children back from their trance. The chamber was opened, and both woke up at the same time. They looked at each other and smiled.

To the children, she was Maggie. It was strange, but it was as if they'd gone to sleep last night, and it was now morning. In fact it was business as usual. The children stood up, and they were not hungry or thirsty. They didn't need to go to the restroom. This was all taken care of like it was some package holiday. The children were not confused in any way. They were ready for whatever the day had for them. Unknown to them, it would be a short visit before they went back to sleep again. This was the only way the children could survive the long journey from Loch Ness to Odessa.

This was not a normal journey. No one in the world had completed a journey like this, from Captain Cook to Christopher Columbus. They were great pioneers, but they had only scratched the surface. This was the real deal.

A large door opened, and Maggie appeared, The children couldn't help admiring her beauty as the princess of the Loch. The children had only seen her outside her outer skin at her palace. Never before had she wandered from her Nessie body outside.

This was her first, and she was excited. She sat the children down and told them of her desire to go onto the sandy shores of Cyprus to walk with them. For Nessie, this was going to be a once-in-a-lifetime opportunity.

Maggie gazed at the children in the way a hen would parade her chicks for the first time. This was what Maggie wanted to achieve – a chance to cherish the moment. The children had probably never heard of Cyprus, but did it really matter? Nessie was experiencing joy, peace, and tranquillity while making history in the sunshine of the Mediterranean. It was a dream come true.

Seonag grasped her hand, which was much easier for a girl; Hamish found it harder to do. With a shy grin, he held out his hand. They strolled across the sandy beach as if they were out on a shopping trip to the mall, setting off at slow pace.

While the three enjoyed the sunset, they could still feel the hot atmosphere and the soft, hot sand. The sun had been up for fifteen hours, causing the beautiful scent of dried seaweed. Maggie looked at the water from a different angle. For most of her life, she had watched the shores of Loch Ness from a distance.

We can be like that many times, when we gaze at the moon and wonder what would it be like there, or what its' like to score winning goals at a World Cup final, or to be a celebrity. These are things that could go through our human minds, with the hope that maybe someday they could come true. For many, it never happens.

This very short journey would last only about half an hour, and then it was back to the mist. Prisoners got more time to exercise than this every day. After several thousand years, Nessie's thirty-minute break sounded sad, but not everyone was the princess of the loch and lived in a palace.

The three headed slowly along the white sands, Hamish kicking shells around him and Seonag sifting handfuls of sand through her fingers. This was so real that most of the things that were free could give children the greatest excitement in life.

In great admiration, Maggie gazed at the hills and the sunset shadowing the surrounds. "What an awesome picture!" The picture changed every moment as the sun disappeared, leaving the shoreline glittering and sparkling like pearls. "What a moment of peace and tranquillity."

There are times that we find ourselves reflecting on the pinnacle moments of our life: our engagement, our wedding, the birth of our first child. Sadly, many never get to that pinnacle ever again. It's like when young people enjoy the intake of alcohol at a young age. That glowing feeling that booze gives makes them laugh and forgot their problems, but it's only for a moment.

Near the end of the beach was a dead-end with a cliff, preventing them from going farther. It was time for them to go back. Maggie loved the sea breeze, which was so fresh and new. On their way back, they walked the area above the tide, which was the most used way for commuters while looking for driftwood, bottles containing messages, bits of coconuts, and debris fallen off of a ship.

The sun was almost totally out of sight, and the full moon was coming into view. It's wonderful when you can see the sun and the moon together, one rising and one departing. It is a wee bit like life and death, a circle where there is sadness and joy. They made out the skyline and managed to walk without a flashlight.

After walking one-third of their way, the children noticed a couple in their early twenties sitting on a nearby ridge. Maggie's attention focused on this couple; this was her first encounter with earthly inhabitants, apart from the two children. She continued her pace towards them. The couple was amazed at how Maggie shone in the twilight, and they whispered to each other.

The young man politely spoke. "Who are you?" She didn't look like a tourist. She looked different.

Maggie stopped and replied, "I am Mary of the Loch. Who are you?"

"We are on our honeymoon," replied the young boy, who did all the talking.

Nessie then asked, "What is a honeymoon?"

The boy was stuck for words for a second, and then he tried to explain. "When a man falls in love with a woman, and the two get married, this is the next stage. The married couple goes on a romantic holiday."

Nessie thought, *We dinosaurs just got on with it.* "Are you from here?" she asked.

"No. We are from Oban in Scotland."

Upon hearing this, the children weren't excited because of the limitations of their mind.

The young man's wife who had said nothing the whole time, picked up her small camera and took a picture. The flash shocked Maggie, who wasn't familiar to human activity. She gazed at the apparatus that millions of people used to try to picture her.

"Who gave you permission to take that picture?" Maggie uttered with annoyance. She knew that her privacy had been breached, and all she could do was to walk to her mist with the children. However, she couldn't help but glance back at the couple. "What will you do with the picture?" she asked. There was no reply.

Again, Nessie felt that landing in Cyprus may have caused some more problems. She got the children aboard and disappeared back into the ocean with a compass bearing, heading for Odessa.

The couple tried to follow the threesome from a distance, but all of a sudden there was no sign of the strangers. The beach wasn't large; it would be impossible to hide. They couldn't believe that the three had suddenly disappeared.

After wandering down to the sand, they saw the footprints along the path that reached one area close to the sea. But to their amazement, the footprints stopped at the tide mark. If the footprints had continued to the sea, then there was an option that they had swum away. But the distance between the footsteps and the ocean was about one hundred feet. The couple turned around and made their way to their hotel, which overlooked the sea. It was late, and it was time to call it a day.

Back in the ocean, Nessie was heading to the last part of the long journey. The children were once again in a trance. Possibly the next time they woke up, they would almost be at the orphanage of their dreams.

Nessie was aware that pictures were used to show people around the world and be sold to newspapers. Nessie knew that these pictures taken on the shore with the children may soon be worldwide. This was different. Her picture with two humans in a foreign country? This could not be allowed to happen. It would be a disaster should they go public. Leaving her Nessie body outside the palace was against the dinosaurs' most rigid laws. What now? Where did she go from here? Facing the naval submarine dam with this on her mind could distract her and cause her to fail. It was a dilemma that needed imminent attention.

17

KNOWING THE DEPTH OF LOCH NESS
and its width wasn't lot for them to go on. Even the
pictures were not concrete evidence of her existence. The
truth was there was no evidence to prove that she was a
female or a male. When the journalists and the press couldn't
understand something, they would make it up.

But this journey had a romantic touch. Unknown to
the world, she was a dinosaur. The people never saw her as a
dinosaur. Everyone had a completely different opinion.

Many years ago, she'd had a relationship with another
dinosaur, called Uisdean. To the world, she was Nessie.
Maybe this trip to the eastern block would connect them
again. The hope in her heart was that she would meet her old
friend once again, and their union would produce the golden
egg, which would carry the next generation of dinosaurs.

The human brain couldn't understand that Nessie may one day die.

She brought great wealth to the Hebridean hamlets close to Loch Ness and for the rest of Scotland. The fulfilment of the golden egg would be the icing on the cake, and delivering Hamish and Seonag would be a wonderful way for Nessie to close the book on this journey.

The young couple was up early to get the camera film developed, and to prove to themselves that it had really happened. This was mainly to prove that their minds were in good condition. They stopped for coffee and toast by the bay overlooking the beach, where they had encountered the trio. The young couple brought the film to a chemist store to get developed; this would take some time. They desired to see the scenery to kill time.

They were on honeymoon, and love did mess with their minds, but at this moment they wanted to prove that they were not insane. Unable to settle down, the young couple started to walk back to the chemist. The couple paid what was due and hurried to the Burnside Cottage Tea Room next to the bridge that was close to the shore. so they could view the prints. With excitement they ordered two coffees and two scones and then sat in a quiet corner of the tearoom.

One by one, they began to view the cluster of twenty-five prints. The first few were their wedding photos, but they were more interested in the previous nights picture. When they came to the last picture they held their breath and couldn't believe what they saw.

"It wasn't the beautiful woman who looked like an angel.

The two children are clear as a bell. How could a beautiful woman look like a monster?" they whispered in disbelief. They put the pictures away and then looked at them over and over. The girl in the cafe was staring at them and sensed that there was something strange going on.

"What do we do now? Shall we share this with someone, or keep it a secret?" The couple decided to go back to the hotel to shower because the weather was very hot, and what they'd discovered had blown their minds.

They felt fresh after a shower and headed down to the local bar for a soft drink. They kept in total silence, only staring at each other. Finally they said, "Where do we go from here?" They picked up a tabloid paper and gazed at each other again. The same thought ran through their minds: Money. Dollars. Was this a bad idea? They knew the main tabloids back in their own country, and they remembered the hullabaloo that had been in the papers some time ago with the headline "Monster Mania". Several articles talked about a monster that was sighted off Loch Morar went viral, then an oil rig, and then two boats off Barcelona.

All of a sudden, the girl let out a scream, and the whole place stared. They both left. "What's wrong?" her husband asked.

Hysterical, she said, "What if she was the monster in disguise?" "No way," replied her husband. They settled down and decided to walk on the beach.

"How much do you think this picture could be worth? If the press knew, would they believe that this monster was a beautiful damsel with silver hair and glamorous beauty?

That is hard to explain," said the wife. In their greedy heads and deep down, they knew they had a photo of the monster. But who in the world were the children?

There was something different in this picture. Although it looked like a monster, it was lifelike. It looked peaceful and happy, but who would believe them? After looking at it again, they both could sense that somehow the picture was talking to them, saying, "Please keep it a secret." At times, they envisioned the monster was crying. Soon they hid the photo underneath their clothes inside the suitcase, as if they had stolen something. Then they realised that it wasn't theirs.

Amazed with what was going on, they looked at each other. The exciting thought of selling the picture gave them a guilt trip. The monster seemed to have been embedded in their hearts, and they knew that until they did something right, they would never get peace. It was a scary thing when one was feeling guilty, and this guilt trip could only be rectified when a solution was found. At that moment, they weren't there yet.

Instead of going to the bar and asking for a stiff drink, they settled for a cup of cocoa and some shortbread. Then they headed to bed for an early night savour. Their past experience, which would have been a great excitement, now became a big question mark hanging over them. They felt scared to go to the bottom of the suitcase to get one last glance at the photo. For the second night of their honeymoon, they lay back and fell asleep and within seconds into complete unconsciousness.

Unexpectedly, their sleep was disrupted by a bright light

shining in the room. Believing it to be the rising sun, they glanced at their watches and noticed that it was only 2:00 a.m. The bright light brought no fear to them. Then they saw a beautiful princess sitting on the edge of their window – the same princess they'd seen at the beach.

She smiled at them and said, "Apologies for the intrusion at this hour." The couple peered without blinking and listened to the soft voice as she spoke with tears on her cheek. "The photo," she said in a gentle, low voice. "It shows my real identity, who I really am. I ask you tonight to destroy the photo. Otherwise, it will destroy me, as well as my ancestors and what they stood for all these thousands of years. You will destroy the innocent children that were with me. I will let you in on a secret. These children were Scottish. They were on a mission to find the orphanage of their dreams. Please don't ruin it for them as well. We are at your mercy. I cannot stop you. If you destroy the picture, I will protect you for the rest of your lives. The whole experience on the beach and the camera must not be brought up in public or private conversation. But you must promise it ends here. I know that money could make you rich, but you would not be happy. However, if we close the book tonight, your life will start fresh from this hour."

They both got out of bed and looked Maggie in the eye. A few moments later, the young man opened his bag and took out the photo. Without looking at his wife, he tore up the picture. Maggie opened the window, and the pieces of photo vanished, as did the princess.

The couple did not go back to bed but instead put on the

kettle. They knew in their hearts that the secret had to be kept for the rest of their lives. We all have secrets. Wouldn't it be great if we kept all secrets? But sadly when secrets are not kept, the ugly world of gossip takes over.

The next morning, it was time for them to return to Scotland. As they waited for their taxi to arrive, they looked at the beautiful beach, where many people were playing. The sun was giving its full heat to the place.

The taxi pulled over in front of, them and a very polite Cyprian man opened the door of a limousine for them. They looked at each other in dismay, and within seconds the sandy beach disappeared.

As they sat waiting for the plane to take off, the air hostess approached the couple. They thought they had done something wrong, but she smiled and said, "Sir and madam, you have been upgraded to first class." They looked at each other in shock. Within thirty minutes they were enjoying a lobster and salmon meal. It was like a valve in their hearts would not allow them to talk or speculate about the previous night.

Upon arriving back in Oban, as they entered their home, they saw much unwanted mail The husband opened an official letter and found that it contained a job promotion. When he'd left for his honeymoon, he thought he was going to lose his job. His wife was on the sofa, opening her mail. She let out a huge scream after reading the results of a test. She was pregnant. Previously, she was told she could not have children. Deep in their hearts was a third person they would never forget, who reminded them that money could make them greedy. Because they kept their promise, they were receiving their full reward beyond measure. They promised each other to return each year, as a pilgrimage. They'd walk the sandy beach at night. In their living room was a large picture of Loch Ness. It was part of the family.

18

AS NESSIE MOVED FARTHER FROM Cyprus en route to Odessa, she reflected on the sand walk with the children. Sadly, she knew in her heart that it would be her last.

In less than four hours, she would be within thirty miles of the shores of Odessa. The water was getting colder the farther she got from Cyprus. Very soon she would have to prepare to dive. Her crew would be briefed on their duties. During drilling, a massive drill with a diamond bit was required for drilling hard rocks. She would encounter many different lairs of shale. Some layers would be soft, some were gas, and there was also oil and mud. These all would bring their own problems.

Her hidden drill was close to her brow. It would be used for drilling with the diamond bit attached. Also, she had a circular saw two metres bigger than the breadth of her body.

The teeth of the saw were made of special reinforcements capable of cutting through anything. It was a tall order, but this was the plan.

They'd drill well outside the radius of the secret naval submarine base to a depth of half a mile. Then they'd drill a mile and a half horizontally and half a mile up to arrive in the basin of the base and surprise those in charge. They'd blow the base up to protect the secrets of the high-tech submarines, so Nessie could get entry to the lake to visit Uisdean. She hoped they could produce the golden egg and allow the children to fulfil their own dream.

As she neared the area, she would dive shortly and have to drill at a forty-five-degree angle. When she reached the sea bed, there were strong tides in the area. Having dynamic positioning was a great advantage to reaching her target. This tunnelling would be so different to the previous tunnelling at Loch Ness. This one had to be dug.

In the last few weeks, unknown to the world, she had shredded ninety-eight stones in weight for the tunnelling. If one weighed twenty-four tons, one could afford to lose that much weight!

It was time. Archie and Betty were strapped on board. She started to sink slowly. It would take twenty minutes to get to the sea bed. Long stalks of seaweed bounced of her body. Jellyfish sprawled over her face. She slowed down to almost stationary. Getting into position with strong tides was precarious, but dynamic positioning helped to stabilise her on her decent. Prior to reaching the area around the base, she had a satellite positioned above the base to indicate whether there were any alerts at the navy base regarding activity in her area.

There was no time to waste. She was ready to spud in, using a terminology in oil drilling. The drill was released and projected about four meters . The circular saw would work in conjunction with the drill. All the mud, stones, oil, and coal would go through Nessie's stomach system. It was Archie's job to make sure the large rocks were broken prior to reaching her stomach. Betty watched all the medical issues and had a few indigestion pills for an upset stomach, just in case.

All systems were in operation. The oil sprinklers were pouring oil through her pores to prevent sticking in the area that had been drilled. The depth of drilling would have to be at forty degrees for half a mile down, then one and a half miles horizontal, and then half a mile upwards at forty-five degrees. This should bring Nessie to the centre of the basin in the middle of the naval base, if her maths was right.

The first layer was reasonably soft. Oil was applied through the centre of the drill to prevent it from sticking. Archie was receiving the first drilling stones. They were coming through the digestive system, and the excess was allowed to be released through the gills and was eventually pushed behind.

This was hard on Nessie. Archie made sure the bigger stones were broken prior going through the gills. Things were going well. They now reached some really hard rock, which slowed the process. Nessie's teeth were struggling to crack the larger rocks; let's not forget she had lost a tooth on her travels. Heat was a big problem, with only a small portion of oxygen being circulated through her nostrils and gills ; it was important to save as much oxygen as possible. They also had to deal with the dust. This was an issue, but as long as Nessie went forward and did not cause any concern for the base, things were good.

Eventually softer shale approached, which would make drilling easier, but that made Archie's job harder. They drilled for fifty hours, with only five hundred metres to the turn and then easier drilling. Directional drilling would be used for the first forty-five-degree angle, to get through the first bend.

After four more hours, she had drilled beyond the bend and was now on the vertical route. There was no turning back, no stopping A gas pockets showed its ugly head and could be very dangerous.

If Nessie's ancestors knew what was happening, she would be grounded. Two hundred metres to go. It was soft shale, soft enough to retrieve the drill. Soon she would be coming to the sea bed. The base was not aware of any movement. A moment would come that she would allow herself to be identified, but not yet. At one hundred metres to go, it was time to crawl up to the surface.

19

ARCHIE AND BETTY HOPED THAT THE last task was successful, and that they would be allowed to return to their graves from thousands years ago. After being traded for two children who would not survive the journey inside Nessie, and after carrying out their duties, the old dinosaurs had little control over their borrowed time. The two dinosaurs were a large part of the plan.

Nessie prepared herself from the start of the journey for the attack on the base. She had to be ready because there was no room for error, even though at the back of her mind she knew things did not always go as planned.

She wasn't totally aware of the havoc she'd caused on her journey from Loch Ness to the other side of the world. Nessie did not read papers, text on a phone, or use Twitter. She soldiered on with business as usual. Unknown to her, the world had a deep love affair with her. Many children did not see her as a monster but as a cuddly friend they wanted to meet. Shortly, the naval base would find out how much of a cuddly friend she was. Upon spotting her in the loch, many children would like their dreams to come to pass. They may not be as fortunate as Hamish and Seonag, but then, who would want their upbringing?

Cutting through the final layer of shale just before breaking into the surface to the seabed was much easier.

The long hours of tunnelling with poor visibility and poor conditions had been very hard. Getting stuck would have been a disaster. She slowed the pace. Breaking the surface would have to be done with little disturbance. This was not the time to be discovered. A time would come that she'd allowed herself to be discovered, but not yet.

For Archie and Betty, it was time for real action. This was the main reason for which they were brought back. Nessie upgraded the bold heroes for the final battle. Both of them changed into fighting soldiers. Archie was changed into a tall, good-looking, broad-shouldered man equipped with a sword, with the ability to use it at high speeds so that those who came up against him would believe that they had come up against a small army, not a single soldier.

Betty had an active role that would turn her into a woman of valour, and she was equipped with the same ability as Archie. She no longer was timid, but was a cunning fighter. Her ability to use a sword would be second to none. She used it as if she had done so every day of her life.

Both were now ready for the call, and when the operations started, it would be all hands on deck. The battle would be fought with Nessie doing the least in her team. Of course, she carried the whole responsibilities if things went wrong.

The drilling stopped as she slowly broke into the seabed. It was very hard for a monster like Nessie to make little noise. This area was a place that naval personnel would not expect any enemy or intruder to appear. This was not a part on which they would focus. No one turned up in the basin undetected. Although the tunnelling was complete, a deserved break could be in order. However, she went straight into the battle.

Nessie hadn't fought before against gunfire, which was different from the old days when it was muscle strength and persistence until they brought results.

The clock was ticking fast, and the mission had to work in sequence, not in confusion. Eventually she hoped to get within the dam and make her way up the loch. There was no other way without the destruction of the naval base.

There was still a trick up Nessie's sleeve. Down in the bulges of her body, she had a very important cargo which would be part of the invasion. The bulges were usually found in a ship or oil rig. It was where most of the waste oil was gathered, but this was different. This weapon had never been used outside of Scotland. It was one the Scots were very proud of. However, the weapon has a downside: it could turn against its own people.

Inside the bulges were forty million half-starved midges, quietly asleep. When heated at a certain temperature, they would come alive and be ready to cause havoc to the naval base personnel. No matter who had previously attacked this naval base, this would be the first attack by midges. The midges were in bags attached to Betty and Archie. After surfacing and just prior to scaling the dam, the bags would automatically burst. The midges would attack the naval base personnel.

Midges were found near water or marshes. There were three kinds of midges. They were annoying and usually irritable, but they were not dangerous except when they left home against their will and weren't regularly fed.

Nessie was now ready for battle. She moved close to the dam with a signal to her two heroes. Archie and Betty were loosed. They swam to the dam and made their way up the side using magnetic pads to scale the sixty-inch-thick steel, which protected the concrete of the dam. As they started the steep climb, the bags of midges burst. The midges would arrive four minutes before Archie and Betty. Nessie swam into the centre of the basin, just below the surface. The operation was now in motion.

The naval base noticed that something was up. Never before was there an alert. There was panic as personnel looked at each other, and then they heard six bangs around the dam. Was someone trying to blow it up? There was no sign of destruction, and the dam was still intact, but whatever was going on was not business as usual. The shift was about to change, with the night shift preparing to come off and the day shift preparing to come on.

The soldiers headed towards the areas they believed were being attacked. Suddenly, they heard a hissing noise that got louder. It sounded like geese, but when they examined the sky, there was no birds in sight. Without warning, they saw a cloud heading towards them. There was nothing big enough to shoot at. Within seconds they were engulfed by insects that started to tear at their bodies.

The dam was the last thing on their minds. The soldiers had scores of these insects attacking them. Eventually some of the soldiers endured so much pain that they jumped into the basin and tried to keep both their heads and hands below the water.

The shift change was routine until this morning, when they were invaded by insects that started to come through the open windows, under the door, and through the air vents. As the soldiers tried to protect their bodies, it was almost impossible to be professional and fight.

The headquarters was also struck with a wave of midges. Within a short time, no one was in control. Everyone was fighting for his own life. Never before in their lives had they been attacked with vicious insects.

The commander-in-chief gathered intelligence to get information on how to proceed. "This was not an air attack by plane or by sea! But where did these bangs from the dam come from?" No one was able to investigate the bangs at the dam. Eventually, when things could not get worse, they saw an object in the basin. It was impossible for something to get into basin unnoticed. It was as if the whole operation was controlled by what was within the basin.

The soldiers who made it to the shift change found the headquarters deserted. All they could see was soldiers and sailors trying to save their own lives.

When they believed that they were getting on top of things, they noticed what looked like an army with swords. It was hard to make out how many people were in the attacking army. They were ordered to shoot to kill with round after round of ammunition. The army kept coming towards the headquarters.

The base now believed that they were being fought on all fronts. They were renowned for their fighting spirits, but this was something different. Nessie was controlling the whole operation from the middle of the basin. She was also aware the life span of the midges was almost finished. If the headquarters realised this, the soldiers may feel that they were winning the battle. Nessie was worried that the base had not panicked enough to blow up the inner dam. She had no more tricks up her sleeves. Well, there was one.

After the long days and hours of tunnelling, Nessie had built up trapped wind within her. She decided to raise herself up from the basin and release an odour to make life easier for her but not easier for naval personnel at the base. A gaseous wave slowly moved around the base, and within minutes, the gas detectors around the base started to go off. The smell, which came in waves, was the most dangerous yet.

The headquarters called for an emergency meeting and was briefed on the latest attack. They came to the conclusion that the strong odour was a chemical attack that could kill all in minutes. It would be shameful if they all died and allowed an unknown force to take over. By now, the special meeting was in chaos with coughing and splattering. Unknown to them, the midges had lost their grip, but this new invasion

led the commander-in-chief to announce, "We have no
option but to blow the whole site, to prevent all the secret
plans from getting into enemy hands."

Nessie looked at the innocent starry sky. This was not a
time to get emotional. Within a split second, the sky lit up,
and the inner dam burst in three places.

"Yes!" Nessie happily muttered, although she was not out
of the woods yet The swirling water was round her, and parts
of the submarines flew dangerously beside her. She kept her
position by dynamic positioning as the severe force of water
surrounded her. She held tight and eventually would be able
to get through to the lake, which was her original plan. She
knew the water round the dam would be very hot, but within
an hour it would be safe.

The water cooled off, but she could not swim under
where the dam was in case she got stuck in the debris. "There
is no security left. Now I can safely swim on the surface
without being detected," she believed. How wrong Nessie
was! She knew of a place where she could rest. About three
miles underwater, there was a ledge under the cleft of a rock.
She would be safe there for the time being, but she couldn't
stay there forever.

20

NESSIE KNEW THE LAKE VERY WELL. She knew the cleft of the rock well, where it was safe to catch her breath. Very soon the lake would be swarming with high-ranking personnel who would try to piece together what went wrong, who did it, and what for. The whole thing was bamboozling. They knew that the world media wanted answers. The world's greatest intelligence agency made the base many years ago. It was impossible to enter into the basin either by sea or by land; there was no way in.

The cave had no home comforts. It was three miles underwater, and of course, it was not like her standards in her palace in Loch Ness. However, beggars couldn't be choosers. Once the activity on the surface calmed down, she would come to land, and hopefully if Uisdean was alive, he would smell her scent – not Chanel No. 5, but something much stronger, more expensive, and more precious.

All her life, whenever there were dinosaur wars, she did not have to hide three miles underground. This situation was entirely different. She'd defeated one of the greatest armies of the world. The next twenty-four hours was crucial for Nessie. An outer space satellite had shown the devastation of the dam to the world media, or else the world would have no idea that such a place existed. What was the country hiding?

Odessa was to give a statement within hours. They were pressured to come clean and leave no stones unturned. That evening the whole world waited for a press conference. Eventually, the spokesman started by telling the world, "What they had at the base was for training submarine personnel and testing submarines. The present situation is a total mystery."

He paused for a moment and went on regarding the plague of insects found floating in the dam debris. Samples were taken for scientists to analyse. "The insects were not from this country but from Scotland, possibly from the west coast. These insects, called midges, on record do not normally bite viciously, and definitely not so severe as to attack on the naval personnel. As we pondered on this situation, we wondered that they may have been starved for this specific job.

"A sample of the air was sent to be analysed for whether it was a chemical attack. I feel embarrassed and shameful to tell you after analysing the gas that the gas was nothing more than a universal human experience, commonly known as breaking wind. In fact, one of the scientists said if they had this gas during the last civil war, it would be over in six months.

"Finally, we have one CCTV camera left hanging after the devastation, and it picked up an animal or creature that was hard to make out due to the damage done in the area of the camera. We believe that this is the monster that caused havoc throughout the world. It is now within our waters, and once we get clearance within forty-eight hours, the lake will be poisoned with the hope of ridding the world of this creature. We still can't establish the army that came from the dam, and no matter how many rounds were fired at them, none fell. It was as if they were transparent. They kept coming, and the closer they came, the fewer there seemed to be – but there were no bodies lying dead on the ground.

"At this time, the foul smell was detected, and the gas detector went off. A ruling was made that the secret base was under siege, and the country's secret service was in danger. The decision was made to blow up the inner dam with all submarines and high-profile equipment. I believed at that time it was the right decision. There was no aerial attack, and neither was there a sea attack. Nothing like this has happened, not even in any world wars.

"Who was this monster? Who was behind it? Where was she heading? And more important, where is she right now?" asked the confused spokesman. "We have great regret for all who loved the loch and its surroundings. Very soon it will be out of bounds due to the poisoning, which will kill all fish and all animals associated with the lake. At the moment, we are on high alert, and the frightening issue is where will this monster will strike again."

The journalists throughout the world who attended were

astounded. They had been to many press conferences, but never one like this one. Many of these journalists followed disasters, wars, and elections, but never had they come across anything like this.

"We believed that a monster left Scotland and for some reason wanted into this lake. For what reason, we may never know. But we cannot take the chance of allowing it to roam the world. We hope that it will die by poisoning, which hopefully makes the world go back to normal."

A journalist stood up with a bit of humour to the story. "All we need now is haggis, and a kilt, and we could have St. Andrew's Day in Odessa."

21

THE ATTACK WAS THE TALK everywhere. People were trying to put together the story in their own minds. What saddened the world was that this monster was going to be poisoned. Groups of animal rights activists, and those involved in the authority of fishing, protesting the lake being poisoned. The act would cause the death of thousands of fish – and possibly the death of a monster whom the whole world loved.

There was no concrete evidence that this was the Loch Ness monster, only speculation. But what many TV presenters and analysts asked each other was how could a creature so timid and a great attraction to the world leave its habitation and go nuts? Many speculated that this had nothing to do with Loch Ness, given that it was all the way from the coast of Scotland to Barcelona, the oil rigs, the fishing boats, and now the base.

When this latest breaking news developed, saying that she was going to be killed, there was an outcry. But for the bed and breakfasts and the hoteliers, their outcry certainly wasn't for poor Nessie, but the fact that next season their bank balance may not be so attractive. They may not be able to spend the three winter months in Monte Carlo or Florida.

It was time for Nessie to move from her watery abode and face the world. Although it was very dark on the ledge, she knew that on the surface, light was fading. Being huddled on the ledge for a period of time made Nessie very sore. She wasn't getting any younger. With sadness, she wondered whether her time was running out. Maybe it was too late for the golden egg. She would know by sunrise whether Uisdean was around, and if he was up for it. He was much older, by 250 years.

She slipped off the edge, stretched, and moved herself under the ledge until it was clear to make her way to the surface. Once she got within half a mile of the surface, she would be able to pick up any signals of danger. Sadly, this was not Loch Ness, where her only problem was tourists and seagulls. This was a difficult time in her life, with a whole army possibly against her.

She came to the surface slower than normal, which enabled her to scan the lake. As she came out of the water and pulled sluggishly unto the dry land, she drained herself. This wasn't something that she did on a regular basis. The last time she went ashore was on the oil rig, and previously her landing on Loch Ness. She made her way to a small hill, hoping to pick up Uisdean's scent.

She watched the full darkness close the curtain on the evening. *If Uisdean is alive, he should have got my scent by now,* she thought. *He wouldn't be playing hard to get because he is the only male dinosaur left*

The night was cold. Nessie wasn't used to the cold weather. She spent a lot of her time in her palace, which had a temperature with which she was comfortable. She listened and watched. *Still no scent of Uisdean.* Nessie sighed longingly. As the night went on, each minute felt like an hour.

All of a sudden, a strong sensation came to Nessie signifying that Uisdean was around. Although she could not see him, she felt the scent getting stronger and stronger. She can now see a shadow coming through the mist until she could make out the face of her long-time friend.

He smiled a dinosaur smile. He had lost weight and looked very old. His outer beauty was gone. Mind you, the last time she had seen him was 150 years ago. Uisdean was now a pensioner. A dinosaur pension started at three hundred years of age.

He came near her and looked her in the eye. He stared at her for a moment and then shook his head. "What in the world have you done? Not a very romantic welcome. It is too dangerous for us to be here. Follow me."

There was no arguing. She followed him, and within minutes they were within the lake. Nessie swam close to Uisdean. The water was murky with little visibility. They went deeper, and then he slowed down for her to catch up.

Eventually Nessie was led to an opening underwater

where there seemed to be a little light. As they came to the entrance of the home, they had to pass stalactites and stalagmites. The entrance to the home looked more like a museum. It was not like the palace she was used to, but she forgot that Uisdean was male.

They both decided to settle on a beautiful cushion with surroundings as if the furniture was cut out from the rock. It was breathtaking. Uisdean prepared to speak, this time with a little tolerance. "You were spotted by the one remaining CCTV camera. You have caused havoc since you left home. Why come now?"

22

UISDEAN TRIED TO OPEN THE conversation with a bit of sensitivity. His thoughts were serious regarding what had happened at the dam. He referred to her as Maggie; he never knew her as Nessie. Many years ago, Maggie was his old girlfriend; they were on and off for over a hundred of years.

Uisdean went on. "The CCTV was not very clear, but it was clear enough for the authorities to believe that you were the one causing havoc all around the world."

Uisdean looked at her in a solemn way, and he made it clear to her that for many years, he and her ancestors never caused any bother with the humans. "But now we have this." Almost in tears, he went on. "I love this country. No one knows me, only the fish and the otters. And now they're all about to be killed."

Maggie looked at him as if in shock. Uisdean became very serious.

"Within forty-eight hours, they're going to poison the lake to kill you. And not only you, but all these friends that use the lake and have lived here for hundreds of years."

She was silent. Silence can be worse than shouting. It gives time to think, to build up another attack. Deep inside her, Maggie knew that the plan went a wee bit wrong.

She believed she had achieved the two main reasons for her to come to Odessa. One was to make a union with Uisdean that would allow the golden egg to be produced, preserving dinosaurs' existence. This one was still in motion. Secondly, she'd fulfilled the promise to two children who were desperate to reach the Orphanage of Dreams.

Maggie was determined to put her case to her friend and hope he would understand why she came, as well as why so much problems arose. She was not going to let him scold her without a fight.

She began her defence. "One night while patrolling Loch Ness in stormy weather, I got entangled with an anchor and chain. I struggled for many hours to make it back to my palace in the loch. The anchor was embedded in my chest, close to my large flipper. The chain was wrapped round my flipper in a way that I was not able to use it.

"I lay there in my palace for almost eight years, alone, with no one to turn to. I had nothing to ease the pain, and I knew for the first time that I was dying. Even at my low ebb in life, I was sure my work on planet earth was not finished. My hope was almost gone, but as you know, we dinosaurs never give up. This time I was very close, unable to get out of my outer Nessie skin. If I died, the palace would eventually be discovered.

"One evening as I rested amidst the pain, I had a dream. It was a strange dream and felt so real. It was as if I was there. I also felt I was going to overcome this problem. When I came to, the dream was very much alive, still in my mind. I lay there thinking, and I knew this dream was very dangerous. It was well outside the dinosaur regulations. But deep inside, I felt the dream was so real that I needed to believe it, and if I didn't act on it, I would possibly die."

Uisdean butted in. "What is the dream, and what did you see?"

She stared at him. He was still agitated about her coming but was now interested in the reason of the dream. She said, "I saw two human children, like the ones who come to get a glimpse of me in the summer. They looked kinder than the adults. They didn't have any cameras, and I don't think they were out to get a million dollars for me, dead or alive. I thought these people loved me for who I was.

"The two children were very young. The boy had red hair, freckles, and short trousers, and he was about the age of nine. The girl was about the age of seven and had long pigtails and wavy red hair. They were by the shore, and then I saw myself abandoned at the edge of the water. The children came to my help. The boy disappeared, and the girl talked to me in the Gaelic language. Although she was frightened, she was still gentle and kind with her words. Then her brother returned with a gadget to help me. He attached it to part of the chain and then asked his sister to tell me to move into another position. By doing this, the anchor and chain were released from my flesh, and I felt free again. Not free from the pain, but free from the bondage of being trapped for the last eight years. The relief was tremendous. I then woke up to find out that the chain and anchor were still there. But in my heart, I felt there was a way out.

"I decided to follow the dream. It happened that way. The children who helped me were the ones in the dream. The strange part of this is that the two children were on their way to Odessa to find the Orphanage of Dreams. It was not possible for them to get there. I felt it was not possible for me to be released from my bondage until I had the dream fulfilled. These children had a dream to get away from their addictive parents and search for the Orphanage of Dreams.

"Very quickly, I realised the orphanage was close to where you lived. I would never have come if I had not made a promise to the children for saving my life, and at the back of mind you were there. Yes, we had several encounters on the way. Much of this was due to the severely damaged flipper. Let's not forget one thing: it was not I who blew up the dam – it was the humans!"

Uisdean was taken aback with her strong Scottish attitude. He shook his head regarding the egg and said, "You're not the real Maggie, and you're no spring chicken! You're off your head,! And how do you know about the million-dollar reward."

She smiled. "The humans put a large aerial on a hill by Loch Ness. One of my monitors has picked up a signal from the Alba State Television. Again, this is outside the dinosaurs regulations."

The old dinosaur dropped his mouth wide open in panic. "Maggie, you are not going to tell me those humans are with you?"

Maggie returned a cheeky smile, dictating that they were.

"You mean you polluted your body with humans? How could you?"

Maggie told him, "Get over it. They saved my life."

It was safe in Uisdean's home, but they could not stay there forever – time was running out. While Nessie and Uisdean were in the comforts of his home, the authorities in Odessa were still trying to come to terms with who was behind the blowing of the dam. The media were having the time of their lives. Normal television news regarding wars, scandals, and sports was put on the back burner. The monster story was on every channel, but there was an element of sadness that the lake was going to be poisoned. Young and old throughout the world were horrified that their favourite friend may have been caught up in something that they didn't believe she was capable of doing. Animal rights activists fought with the authorities to postpone the poisoning for a longer period of time.

But nobody was taken responsibility for what had happened, and no country claimed responsibility. There did not seem to be a political issue surrounding it, and as far as they knew, there were no grievances from other countries. How in the world could a creature travel from Scotland, cause all that havoc, and arrive here? And for some reason, she caused the authorities to blow up the dam? Did she bring the small midges? It was scary to think that these little beasts could only be found on the hills of Scotland. How could she have brought them here and guided them to attack the soldiers? There was no answer to this.

Those in high places could sit round the table for weeks or maybe months, and still not be able to figure out how she got within the basin. Who were the two who were fighting with the swords who looked like armies? And what seemed like a chemical attack was only hot air that stank badly. Could a conclusion be found?

Something strange happened worldwide. The attitude of the people had changed over the last few weeks during the time the story unfolded. The story had turned those who had a heart of stone into new people. Life had meaning, and a monster roaming the ocean and causing havoc was news to the world. It took away the corruption the violence, the anger, and the bitterness that people heard every day on television. This story was fresh off the press, and even prisoners in their cells were caught up in monster mania. They were interested in the next chapter.

All their lives, most of them had violent lifestyles. But this story showed them that through their turmoil, there was something they could grasp onto. How true! This story was not important, but what was important was that this story got into their heads. It brought an element of love, a new way to soften hardened criminals. They went to sleep thinking of the reality of a monster going nuts and, of course, blowing up a dam was as exciting as any war movie. Wouldn't it be wonderful if the whole story was given to the press regarding the two children who started the cycle, and if it was carried to the other side of the world? But this part could not be told.

Before Maggie could bring the children back from their sleep, she would have to return Archie and Betty to where they belonged. Before she did that, she praised them for their obedience and the wonderful work they did at the oil rig and during the fishing boats fiasco. She complimented the brave way they fought in the destruction of the dam. It would have not been possible without them. She smiled at them, and then within a split second, they were gone.

Hamish and Seonag could now come to life after their long sleep. This time they would be awake for good. They woke slowly, and when they came to, it was as if they had just gone to bed the night before. This was going to be a sad parting. Never before in Maggie's life had she said goodbye to humans, but these two were different. They were young and innocent, and she felt very much a part of them.

As Maggie prepared to part with the children, she invited them to her parlour in the flight deck, where everything was controlled. The children were excited to see her and all the dials that controlled this wonderful lady. She switched on the screen, and when she got it focused, in the middle was the Orphanage of Dreams. It had been a long road from Cruach na Moine to Odessa. Now they could see what soon would be their new home.

Maggie was curious and asked, "What is the tree doing in the window with decorations?" She found this very strange. She believed trees grew outside, Hamish quickly told her that it was to celebrate Christmas. "What is Christmas?" Maggie asked.

"It is a time we celebrate the birth of Jesus, the Son of God. And if we accept Him as our personal Saviour, we go to heaven," replied Hamish.

Maggie had been very interested in the spiritual faith of the two children. Just then, Seonag produced from her bag a small, worn Bible she had received from her grandma.

"What is that, Seonag?" Maggie asked.

"It is the word of God."

This confused Maggie, and she glanced at the pages. Within a short time she read it all, and within seconds it was on one of her monitors. She could read this now at her leisure. The children were amazed that within seconds, she could memorise the whole Bible and then put it in the monitor. She really was special. But of course, she was the lady of the loch.

Maggie told the children that Uisdean would deliver them within two miles of the Orphanage of Dreams. Uisdean reluctantly agreed. The children looked at her with tear-filled eyes. A love had grown, unknown to them all. A new dawning began. They prepared to leave the headquarters.

Nessie stayed where she was. She watched the children leave, knowing that she would never see them again. This was only for a season. They were now in position, just a few miles from the Orphanage of Dreams. Soon they would be on their own.

When we reflect on why these children decided to make this journey, we see the desperation that surrounded them.

Many children today are in this position. Parents are not aware of the trauma the children go through. We only know the surface of the big picture of addiction in the home. Alcohol is advertised to bring joy and laughter to the world, but has a downside which destroys families. Here we have a story-like setting surrounding two children with a fairy tale ending. But I can assure you that most children from addictive families are not as fortunate as Hamish and Seonag.

The two children looked at each other as if to say, "We are almost there. What's next?" They were on other side of the world, within touching distance of their dream.

They felt Uisdean take off, and it was a bit bumpy. But they had experienced this already, when they were taken from the shores of Loch Ness to the palace. After a period of time, they could feel Uisdean slowing down again. They held each other's hands as they saw a flap being lifted for them to leave. The first thing that hit them was the severe cold and wind. They walked on the uneven cobbles. Back at Loch Ness, they were dressed for the summer, but here they were in winter clothes: boots, jackets, gloves, and scarves.

Nessie had taken care of their needs. The private lives of the children were protected by Nessie. The winter conditions were more severe than the Scottish weather. At least they would not be bothered with midges, if there were any left.

23

A S THE CHILDREN WALKED ALONG THE windy road, their memories of the past were fading fast, and their thoughts on Maggie were no longer there. Their home life was no longer a memory; all their focus was on the Orphanage of Dreams. They noticed a few lights that were scattered among the hill. The surroundings were similar to Scotland.

They heard horses' hooves getting closer, and so they decided to walk on the edge of the road. They were right: it was a family with two horses and what looked like a home-made caravan. There were two adults and three children, and they came abreast of the children, and stopped. The oldest of the three children was a boy around seven, and he jumped out of the caravan and handed the children what looked like cookies. They were warm, as if they'd been recently baked.

With a smile, the family went on their way. Hamish and Seonag enjoyed the friendly welcome to Odessa.

Ahead was a cluster of lights which might be the place they were looking for. They heard children laughing in the distance, and as they got closer, they could see several children making a snowman. Hamish and Seonag wanted to join them, but, they had to be patient; if it was their destination, they would soon be part of that activity.

Light was fading, and darkness was closing in very quickly. When they reached the large building, they saw animal pictures on the side. This is what they saw on the documentary, and it brought smiles to the children, knowing that they had arrived at the entrance of their dreams. They were noticed by several children who had been playing and now ran up to them with a friendly smile. Hamish and Seonag were excited at the welcome from the children. When they reached the door, one of the children ran ahead to tell someone.

Almost immediately a middle-aged woman appeared with a friendly smile, and she asked no questions about where they had come from. All the children who were there in the orphanage had strange backgrounds. Many were from the street, some were from sewers, and all were from broken homes.

The children were brought inside and were introduced to the other orphans. Hamish was renamed Serge, and Seonag was given the name Luba. The two new children did not argue regarding their names being changed; it had to happen this way for many reasons. The children cheered to welcome them to their new home.

The place didn't get many street children from Scotland in Odessa. The other difference was that they weren't aware these two children had travelled from Scotland in a very unusual way. Their timing was good: it was suppertime. This was what they dreamt of: sitting round the table with other children in front of a big wooden fire, a Christmas tree in the corner, and decorations all around the room. This was why they'd left home, and this was why the ridiculous plan had been put into place. The impossible became possible!

The two children who had been brought up in Scotland were now fluently speaking the native tongue of Odessa. Again, this had to happen to prevent confusion. This new life of happiness without a past was wonderful for the children.

Sadly, today many children have many memories of the past, especially when they come from addict families where poverty and bad language were part of the daily routine. And for many years to come, these memories lingered in their lives even as they grew into adulthood.

After supper, it was time to help with the washing up. Then they sat round the fire and sang Christmas carols, followed by Christmas stories. The first hiccup came when it was bedtime. The two children were separated: boys went to one area of the orphanage, and girls went to another area. By 8:30 p.m., they were in bed to get plenty of sleep before schooling in the morning.

Sadly, many children who were brought to the orphanage found it hard to live there because the rules were too strong for them – getting up at a certain time in the morning and having a certain time to go to bed. There were also many rules regarding chores and tidying up round about the orphanage. It was very hard to change a child who had his or her own way. Many had been institutionalised to life on the streets, and it was almost impossible to break that mould.

Many children got sick while on the street, and the vulnerable ones were very often were the ones who stayed. There was nothing more beautiful than when one sees a street child changing into a normal child. This normality was stolen from them almost from birth. Working with these children required very professional, caring, and loving people. Not everyone was structured to bring street children through their childhood and into the teenage years, ready to fly the nest.

Here in the Orphanage of Dreams, Hamish and Seonag found all the qualities for which they'd left home.

There is a wonderful saying that money can buy the best bed in the world, but only God can give you the peace to sleep on it. It's at this time, with one's head on your pillow, that the diversities of life come to memory. It's these memories that make us toss and turn until eventually we get peace to sleep.

Uisdean arrived home. He noticed that Maggie had come out of her outer skin and was sitting on the green grass-like carpet. For the first time in many years, Uisdean decided to do the same. When he appeared, Maggie noticed how old he really was. He still had the outer beauty from many years ago, and he still had some of his red curly hair.

He sat down beside her and smiled as if they were about to go on a honeymoon. His head dropped, and when he brought it back up, his eyes were full of tears. He didn't mix his words and went straight to the point. "The only way we can get round what's happened is that I give my life up for you. I've had a good life and have fulfilled most of what I've come to do. It is time for me to go to the grave with my ancestors."

He held his breath for a moment and said, "Do you think it's possible that we can produce the golden egg and continue the life of the dinosaurs? If it's possible, when the egg is hatched and the young is weaned into maturity and is able to patrol the loch, you can come with me to the grave of our ancestors."

Maggie made a statement that would shock the most daring dinosaur in the world. She didn't want to go to the grave of her ancestors – she wanted to go to where the humans went. "The children have shown me a more exciting place to go, called heaven. I downloaded their little Bible into one of my dials. I feel their God has been with me all along this journey. Maybe this was meant to be." She had learned so much from the two children and what their grandma had taught them about heaven.

Uisdean looked at her in despair and started to walk towards his outer suit without saying anything. Maggie headed towards her own suit.

It was time for them to go through the motion of the golden egg. Producing the golden egg had to be done in private, as adults did. Only time would tell if they were successful. Also, it had to been done in their outer skins. The golden egg would be completed on the shore of Loch Ness.

This was why Uisdean was willing to confuse the authorities into thinking it was Nessie who was dead. This would stop the lake from being poisoned, and they would no longer look for Nessie. She could escape back to Loch Ness.

Within the hour, Uisdean left the home he had lived in for many hundreds of years. It's always sad when you leave your family home, no matter what the circumstances. The memories of a happy home lingers with you for many years. It was painful for poor Uisdean to walk out for the last time. But what he was doing would save the lives of Maggie, all the fish and birds and otters, and whoever attended the lake. Now the golden egg was on a countdown.

Maggie left before Uisdean, who looked around, set a timer, and then pressed a button that would no longer allow any light to come in his home. It was the end of an era; he'd caught up with Maggie. She followed him along the loch side, and then they both slowly submerged. It was dusk, and this was a better time to land. They got out of the lake and made their way to a high hill overlooking the lake.

The higher they went, the greater the view. They reached a patch of green ground that had no snow. There were few words spoken between them. Uisdean looked across the lake, a place he loved very much; he knew it was his last sunset. Maggie was so overcome by the brave decision of her old friend. Uisdean made a motion that he was going to lie down, possibly for the last time. Maggie did the same, and they sat close to each other. Although for many years they'd lived thousands of miles apart, they were still very close at heart.

It was strange that he could choose when to die, unlike the humans who had no say in the matter.

Uisdean had been content to go with his ancestors until a short time ago. Maggie started speaking about the God of the humans and said that she wanted to go there. He asked Maggie to tell him a little more about what humans believed in. She smiled and said that she would send him the download for the Bible. Within seconds, Uisdean's dial had the gospel. He smiled, and strangely his eyes were drawn to a special verse, John 3:16. The old soldier was getting weaker, and with his last words to Maggie, he said, "I believe in the God of the humans." With a weak smile, his eyelids closed, and he was no more.

Maggie pulled a beautiful Scottish bonnet from her secret pouch, wrote on it in Gaelic, and put it on Uisdean's head. If she only knew the problems that this little bonnet was going to cause.

There was nothing to stay for any longer. She had fulfilled her promise to the two children and had gone through the motion to produce the golden egg and keep the future of the dinosaurs alive. She had led poor old Uisdean to the Lord and watched him for a minute or two. Then she turned for the long road home. She slid quietly into the lake and made her way to the area near the dam where the big problem was. She knew that this would be a precarious situation.

As she got closer, she was aware of much activity with the military. All of a sudden, there was a huge explosion farther up the lake, which took the minds of the soldiers off the present situation. They focused on whatever caused this explosion. Maggie smiled. She knew exactly what the explosion was. When Uisdean set the timer, this gave Maggie time to get away, as if he knew the moment she would be close to where the dam was. His old palace exploded so nobody in the human world would ever be able to trace anything about him. For many hundreds of years, he was never spotted; only those affiliated with the lake knew him as a good friend who protected them and cared.

Within a few short hours Maggie was out of the lake and into the open ocean. Her compass was set for Scotland. Mission completed. For Maggie, it was business as usual. This time she was alone. Well, not really – she had an egg that also had a timer, and someday sooner rather than later, there would be a king or queen of the Loch. Very soon she would be able to smell the air of Scotland, and when she reached the green grass of home, she would be able to look to a future bringing up the young of the golden egg that would take over patrolling the lake.

The locals didn't know that anything had changed. Nessie didn't prance about the loch, allowing herself to be photographed every two minutes. People could get tired of her, so the way she operated was to allow the humans to have an element of dreams, which was more exciting for children. This was the way it was, and it would continue that way. Her short appearances were what made her so famous, like Santa Claus.

24

A NAVAL HELICOPTER FLEW LOW OVER the river, close to the hills to see if they could find any evidence of the perpetrator. When the evening came to an end, the helicopter made one last search for the day. "Wait a minute. I can see something which looks like a small hill. It wasn't there earlier!" said one of the crew.

As they descended to have a closer look, they saw what looked like a carcass. After finding a safe area to land, the three men left the chopper to investigate. To their horror and excitement, what they came upon was what they believed they were looking for. Sadly, it lay motionless, as if it had been dead for several hours.

The airmen contacted their headquarters for assistance and urged others to bring a camera crew with them so that evidence could be used to let the world know that the monster that had caused havoc was now dead. They knew it would take some time before assistance could arrive, so they stayed with the carcass, walking around it to look at the uniqueness of its structure. "This creature is extraordinary!" They had never seen anything like it before. But something confused them. On the head of the dead monster was a tartan bonnet. They presumed that it was a flag or something that represented a country where it had come from.

After fifteen minutes, something was happening to the carcass, and the men looked at each other in confusion. "Is the carcass getting smaller, or are our eyes playing tricks on us?" Within a few more minutes the carcass was half its size and continued to disappear! The crew went from excitement to dismay. One shouted, "Look!" Scores of maggots were eating the underside of the creature. They couldn't believe it. How would they explain this event to the officers who came to assist them? As they stared, everything was gone except for the tartan bonnet.

Before they could catch their breath from disbelief, another two helicopters arrived at the scene, one hovering above and the other landing nearby. The three men felt so embarrassed while trying to figure out how best explain the sudden disappearance of the dead animal. The commander-in-chief discerned that something was wrong as he walked towards them. "There is no more monster, only the area that was flattened by the weight of the creature."

The crew's leading officer shook his head and said, "What am I going to report to the headquarters? This looks like another sham for the world to laugh at!"

The little tartan bonnet was the only evidence they

had. One didn't need to be a top lawyer to figure out that the bonnet was Scottish, and possibly made in China. The commander picked up the bonnet and noticed a secret code written inside. At least this was something to go on.

Bad news travelled fast, and this news had already reached the media. The story release from the press was that the monster was found dead, and many believed it was deliberate. As the news spread, no picture was shown because the dead monster supposedly had disappeared except for a tartan bonnet.

How could a dead monster disappear? The world wanted answers. Scotland wanted answers. This was a prized asset, and it was in shambles. This could not be the end to this story. It could not finish in sadness.

While all this went on, Hamish and Seonag were living in the reality of their dream. This was their first real Christmas, and they were in a foreign country, speaking a foreign language and unaware of their long distance from home. The tranquillity they had dreamed about was now a reality.

The evening when the dead monster was discovered, the authorities were forced to make a statement. It was another embarrassing moment, and every country was now in sympathy with them; no fingers were pointed. The poisoning of the lakes was cancelled. This pleased the world media and those involved in the preservation of riverbeds surrounding the lake, but hearing the monster had died was heartbreaking.

However, there was a twist in the story – again. A tartan

bonnet was found on the head of the dead monster's head when it was first discovered. It remained the only part that was not consumed by the maggots. Upon examination of this bonnet, it was discovered that a secret code was written inside. A top analyst in that field examined the code and concluded that it was written in Gaelic, a Scottish language. A gentleman from the island of Barra, from Scotland, was flying to Odessa with the hope he could break the code.

The new wave of information reached the airways around the world and rekindled the hearts of all Nessie's supporters. Could Nessie still be alive? And who was dead? There was a great excitement, but would the authorities allow the media to get close to the truth of what was written?

The Scottish gentleman arrived and was brought to where the bonnet was held, in a secret location. After a short time, he smiled and laughed to himself as Scottish people did. He tried to be serious – let's not forget he was facing the top brass of Odessa.

"It reads, 'Hughe, the love of my heart. Maggie.'"

There was a long pause, and they eyeballed Mr Campbell with confusion, as if to say, "You can't be serious."

The authorities released the latest part of the saga to the media, and within hours this went out to the four corners of the world. Earlier in the day, there was great sadness that the monster may be dead, but now the news was there may be a love story entwined in the whole thing. Did Nessie have a boyfriend? Within twenty-four hours, it had changed the atmosphere. This new twist had brought music to the ears of the world.

Back in Cruach na Moine, as Lachie watched his television and read his local newspaper, it didn't help him sleep any better. Again, his heart was aroused with the thought that if he went to the press and told his story, he would be a rich man. He now felt he had all the evidence he needed for people to believe him. He paused and allowed his mind to clear. "No, it would not be the right thing to do," he mumbled to himself. He switched off his television and finished his cup of, tea which was the strongest drink he'd had for a long time. He crawled into bed beside his wife.

As he lay there for a short time, he thought of how greed could grip the heart, and how he'd probably take this secret to his grave.

The man from Barra in Scotland arrived back on the island, which he'd left a few days ago, to a hero's welcome. Awaiting him were several photographers and journalists. But Mr Campbell said, "Follow me to the creel bar in the capital, Castle-bay." The press conference went on throughout the night.

25

BACK AT CRUACH NA MOINE, DONALD and his wife, Mary, were coming to terms with their alcohol problem. They presumed that the authorities had taken their children away when they were on a alcoholic binge. They were now following a recovery twelve-step program, and they embraced Grandma's example of religiously going to church. Being sober for ninety days was a long time. They battled most of their adult lives with booze. At last they could see the panoramic view of Christian sobriety. It was never too late to put down the bottle for the last time.

At present, it wasn't the right time to get the children back from the authorities. Donald took a job with the forestry commission, and Mary had part-time work in the school canteen. Getting works played a vital role in the recovery program, which served as a very strong backbone to prolonged sobriety. Anyone could have spontaneous periods of being sober, but a man had to take the right fork in the road to maintain sobriety.

One afternoon, Mary had a day off work and found herself at a loose end. She sat on the sofa to watch TV. She roamed the channels but found nothing exciting. She decided to have a look at the selections of videos they had. She stumbled on a video with no label, so she decided to watch it.

It was about a man from an island who had been helping street children in Odessa. The condition of the poor street children was heartbreaking to watch. Where did these children live and sleep? They roamed aimlessly throughout the night. Many of the children had left their parents because of the alcohol addiction.

Mary became engrossed with the story, and for the first time she recognised that their way of life with alcohol was affecting the lifestyle and health of their children. They had left the children to fend for themselves. The Orphanage of Dreams was a sad story, but for those who made it there, their lives changed. It was not immediate, but over a period of time they gained trust, love, and compassion.

Suddenly, Mary figured out that the most recent television story regarding the monster causing havoc was very close to the location of the orphanage. "Maybe it was just a coincidence," she reflected. "What if we were living in Odessa? Would our children also run away?" She paused for a moment, and a bad thought went through her mind. "We all get that from time to time." In order to get this out from her mind, she got up at the end of the video and started to prepare supper.

While peeling the potatoes, her mind wandered again, but this time she left the potatoes and ran straight into the children's room. She first went to Hamish's to check on his piggy bank, and she was surprised to find it empty. Then she rushed to Seonag's room, and hers was empty. Upon opening her children's drawers and searching, she saw Seonag's cardigan at the bottom corner of the drawer, and she found a crumpled map of Odessa. Mary sat down on Seonag's bed and couldn't help her mind wandering.

She got up and made her way back to the kitchen with tears rolling down her eyes. "Are my children in a foreign country?" She'd believed that they were in the care of the authorities, which was bad enough. This would be the first Christmas without their children.

It was nearly Thanksgiving, and a dinner invitation came as a surprise for Donald and Mary. This was the reward of their sobriety. Being invited was a good opportunity to mix with sober people. On that evening, they were seated beside an elderly couple. They had seen them on many occasions but had never any opportunity to converse with them. They started their dinner. In Scotland, eating and talking went hand in hand.

Of course, the main newspaper headline on everybody's lips was the monster that was roaming around and causing mayhem. What made it more interesting was the area of Loch Ness.

It was not a secret that local people did not believe in the monster that lived in the lake. It brought good business to their district, and so they happily went along with the story. But what had happened in the last few months had brought attention to those who did not believe, and it put a question mark on their thinking of Nessie's existence.

The soft-spoken woman told Donald and Mary how one morning on their way to Inverness, they gave a lift to a young man who was making his way to the Drumnadruchit garage. Mary listened intensively as the woman told them, "The young man said that he was going to get a shifter to release a monster at the loch side, who was with his sister." The woman went on to say that she scolded him for telling lies. Her husband saw the funny side, and she went on to tell the young boy, "Why tell lies to someone who's helping you?" Then she added, "So we dropped him off. And with all this paraphernalia about Nessie and Odessa, and all the problems she supposedly caused around the world, I just wonder if there was an element of truth in it!"

Mary butted in quickly with a touch of anxiety. "How old was the boy, and what was he wearing?" Donald's back went up a wee bit, wondering why his wife had asked this question.

The woman said, "About eight or nine years old, ginger hair with freckles. He had a brown jacket and denim shorts."

The conversation stopped there because they had finished their meal. Mary had other thoughts on her mind. From walking to their car until they reached home five miles away, both were in total silence.

It was getting near midnight, and they sat on the sofa drinking hot chocolate. All of a sudden, Mary turned to her husband. "What if that is our son and our daughter mixed up with this monster?"

Donald had a little more understanding and answered his wife, "This is a hard time for both of us. With Christmas coming up, there is a good possibility that we will not have the children. But you must remember it was summertime, and there were many children in the area with ginger hair and freckles who may look very similar to Hamish."

The next evening, Donald agreed to watch the documentary. It wasn't long before Mary could see how her husband was impressed by the change of the children in the Orphanage of Dreams, as well as the damaging effect of alcohol on children. Donald could not hide his frowning face in shame. No matter how alcohol can diminish your brain, any parent must know that overindulgence greatly affects family life, especially the children.

Then Donald spoke. "Maybe it's time to call the authorities about the children."

Mary spoke very quickly, "What if they say they haven't got them? We will be in trouble! Even without alcohol, you can have problems in life, but it's easier to deal with them when sober."

In the middle of all this, Rex the dog would one night sleep in Hamish's room, and the next he'd been in Seonag's. A dog's actions always told a story.

It was getting close to Christmas. Every year the family, which had very little, managed to put a little aside to buy Christmas presents for their children. This year was different. It was their first sober Christmas, but celebrating it without their children meant it was not Christmas at all.

26

WHILE LYING IN BED, MARY, LIKE many people with something on their minds, Mary tossed and turned before eventually falling asleep. Around 5:00 a.m., she heard a clicking sound from their letter box. "How? The postman is not expected for several hours." In Britain, most doors had slots for mail and small parcels, but larger parcels were to be collected at the local post office.

Curiosity took over, and Mary went downstairs and headed for the door. She was surprised to see two parcels on the carpet. After picking them up, she went straight to the kitchen to put on the kettle – a very normal thing to do.

While waiting for the kettle to boil, she looked at the envelopes, checking for their origin. They had no markings but looked official. In an hour's time, Donald would be up, so she thought of opening them before he wakened. After several minutes, she got to the heart of one of the packages. There were two red books with official stamps on each book. She saw Donald's picture. After flicking through to the next book, she found her recent picture attached. Without pausing, she went to open the next parcel. When she eventually got to the second parcel, there were two airline return tickets to Odessa with departure on December 24.

She picked up the tickets and the passports and put them into one of the large pots. *This will be too much for Donald this early morning,* she thought as she discarded the wrappers.

At their quick breakfast, only few words were said. The couple soon made their way to their jobs. All that morning, Mary pondered how she would tell Donald. Two passports and two tickets. Within two days, they would be flying to London and then farther afield. This was far too much to take in before lunch.

Mary clouded her mind with so many questions. "Who in the world did this? Will this lead us to our children? Could this turn out to be the best Christmas yet?" She recalled the conversations they'd had with the old couple mentioning the little boy with the freckles and a monster. Were their children caught up in all of this? There was no way that she could pick up a telephone to tell friends a story like this; it would turn to gossip, and that could be dangerous. This kind of news would travel faster than Facebook and Twitter put together.

Today was Donald's last day because he would be off until after the festive season. Mary worked part time, which allowed her to be home before her husband. It wasn't what she was going to cook for Donald that troubled her, but what was in the pot. "How am I going to explain it to him?"

The door opened, and in came Donald, rejoicing and saying, "That's my work finished until after the festive season!" They sat down for their meal. Mary was quiet throughout their meal, looking for the right time to tell her husband.

Donald made it easier for her as he opened up the conversation. It was about the documentary and the forthcoming Christmas without the children. Almost in tears, he said, "I would give anything to have my kids and show them I am a real dad."

Mary got up and switched off the television halfway through the news.

Donald objected. "Why? We always watch the news."

She looked at him with a serious grin. "Early this morning, I heard the letter box."

Donald butted in quickly. "It's that goat again, who loves playing with the letter box. I wished that neighbour would keep the gate shut." Mary just looked at him. Donald said, "Why? What's the big deal?"

"No, Donald, it wasn't the goat. In fact, it might have been an angel."

"Mary, you're losing your marbles. I thought your sober life would change you," he said in a gentle voice.

"Listen to me, Donald. Two parcels came in through the letter box in the middle of the night." Donald stayed quiet and listened attentively as Mary told the story. The first thing he thought of was debt packages or something that required payments. Instead of telling him, Mary opened the pot that was in the kitchen and pulled out the two red books. She handed one to Donald and opened it. There was his picture on an official passport.

He read, "Donald Stewart McPhee." Then he said, "Nobody knew my middle name, not even my teacher. Only my parents."

She took out the contents of the second package and handed to Donald the airline tickets with there name on it. It was return tickets to Odessa and back to Glasgow. He was speechless. They had no wealthy friends, and they didn't know anybody who would give them something special like this, except the woman down the road who brought scones on a Wednesday.

It was impossible to figure it out, and if they tried, it confused them. They accepted that however it happened, it was the best gifts they'd ever had, apart from their children. They kept looking at the passports many times that evening.

The only time they ever saw London was on postcards and on the television. The only planes they ever saw were the ones flying above their heads. Mixed with excitement and amazement, Donald headed for the loft and brought down an old, battered suitcase which was first used during their honeymoon to the village of Nairn. That trip had been meant to be two nights, but it turned out to be just one because they fell out while in a drunken state. This often happened to people who started their relationship in a bar.

Late at night, they started putting their few belongings into the case. Some needed washing and ironing. If your clothes are cleaned and ironed, you are doing fine; it doesn't matter how expensive they are. Mary was still awake after a while. Donald asked her, "Why are you not sleeping?"

In tears, she said, "I'm frightened to sleep in case it's only a dream."

He put his arms around his wife, which he had not done for many years. Within a short time, they were in the land of nod.

Poor Rex was confused. He looked at the case as if to say, "What in the world is going on? Am I going to be left alone?"

The next morning, Donald asked his neighbour, "Would you please look after the dog for a couple of days?" At festive times, many people left their homes for few days to meet up with family.

"Yes, it's no problem," the neighbour said without asking where they were going. He knew the children hadn't been around for some time, but people in this rural area made up their own minds regarding situations like this – and very often they were accurate. However, this time they were well off-track.

They woke up very early to catch the bus to the next village, where they would get a bus to Glasgow. Both gazed out the window and across the lake. They saw little white horses and a slight breeze. Soon after, they disembarked and were on the larger bus to Glasgow. They quietly sat side by side. Boarding on a plane was enough for their minds.

For this couple, there was never a hope that they would jet to the other side of Europe. Whoever put these parcels through the letter box was too big for them to speculate. That information was for another day.

They arrived in Glasgow. The congestion of traffic and people milling around mesmerised them a bit because they had lived a sheltered lifestyle. Within a short time, they were on a taxi and heading to the airport on the outskirts of Glasgow.

Walking into the airport was unchartered territory. Mary held their suitcase very close to her, and Donald had the tickets. He handed these tickets over for checking with very few questions asked. The suitcase was taken away from Mary, who would have preferred to have keep it. She forgot to realise that this was not going on a bus.

She watched the young man put it on the conveyor belt. With a hysterical voice, Mary asked him, "When do I get it back?" Unknown to Donald, Mary had bought presents for the children in good faith. They were handed their boarding cards and were directed to proceed to gate seven.

Getting seated on the plane was strange, and they kept looking around at the many people. Locking the seatbelt was a struggle. They were taken aback a little at the demonstration of a lifejacket. Donald smiled and said under his breath, "It doesn't look as if they have much faith in the pilot." The door was then shut, and there was no way back.

Within minutes, the plane moved at high speed – it was a white knuckle time. They were flying for the first time, and all of sudden their heads were in the clouds. When the plane stabilised, they were above the clouds and in the sunshine. "But how in the world do we get back down?" Mary whispered to Donald.

They saw a stewardess coming towards them. "What would you like to drink?" she asked.

Donald shook his head and burst out laughing. After all these years of heavy drinking, now someone was offering free booze for an hour! Without any hesitation, they settled for two cups of tea. By the time they were finished with the cups, they'd touched down in London.

The next plane was bigger and with more passengers. After a smoother takeoff, the stewardess offered them lunch and an offer of any drink. This again brought smile to their faces. They enjoyed their lunch, which let them have a nod for a couple of hours.

They were awakened by the pilot. "Within an hour, we will be touching down in Odessa." Very soon they would be in a country that they hadn't even heard of until recently. As they taxied to their gate, there was silence between the two. Mary wondered where her suitcase was. Poor Donald was concerned about how he would manage to speak to foreign people, given that many times he had struggled speaking to his neighbours. Everybody undid their seat belts and headed for the exit. They followed the crowd. Mary was confused about leaving the plane without the suitcase, but it was too late to go back. There was a difference between a bus driver and a pilot. They didn't have the same one to one with the pilot as they had with the local bus driver. Thank goodness for that.

At the immigration counter, the officer asked their business in Odessa.

Donald said, "To visit street children."

The man smiled and stamped both passports.

As they passed him, Mary asked, "Where's my suitcase?" The man answered, but she didn't understand him. They continued to follow the rest of the passengers until they reached the waiting area for their luggage. They noticed several people gathered and looking at a certain conveyor belt. When they got closer, to their horror the people were staring at their antique suitcase, which normally would be seen in an old movie. Mary barged in as if she'd lived there all her life, and she picked up the tattered suitcase.

She and Donald made their way to the exit. They were exhausted because it had been a long day: the buses, the taxi, and two planes. Now they were waiting for another taxi.

27

THEY COULD FEEL THE DIFFERENCE OF
their surroundings as they waited in the taxi rank, with
people speaking different languages. They boarded an old,
shabby taxi, the driver recognised straight away that they
were not from his country. It was the first time the McPhee's
had spoken to a foreign person, apart from customs. Speaking
pidgin did not come naturally.

Instinctively, Mary decided to be the spokesperson.
She had written the street of the Orphanage of Dreams
on a piece of paper prior to leaving home. She handed it to
the driver, and he answered back, "I know Dr Ramo. Very
good man. Many street children in big house." Donald was
impressed with his wife as they sat close together, comforting
one another. They were far from the islands and the people
with whom they grew up. This was not a night to fall out,
stop the taxi, and walk home – a situation which happened

in their days of binge drinking. Tonight was different, and they needed each other more than ever.

People were wrapped up for the winter months as cold temperatures hit the country. People walked in a hurry. Streets were dark and very bumpy. As they got nearer the city centre, they saw many children on both sides of the road, and few had adults with them.

"Many children, no mama, no Papa. Where they stay?" Donald queried the driver.

The driver understood him and clearly said, "The children have no home due to their parents drinking too much vodka. They feel safer living underground. During the day, they come up to beg for food. At night they disappear into warm holes underground."

Mary and Donald were silent and thinking the same thing. "If we had lived in Odessa, would our children have run away?" Their children were farther away from home than these local children. It was hard for them to believe that booze could damage a family so much. Mary and Donald felt shame and looked at the taxi floor in silence. Mary wept silently. The long day was catching up to them, and they had seen firsthand what alcohol could do to young children who preferred to sleep in a smelly sewer than live with their parents.

The taxi slowed down, and the driver lowered the window for a clearer vision. They had arrived at the Orphanage of Dreams. After handing over foreign currency and a tip for the driver, Donald and Mary stood on the pavement with excitement as they reached another milestone of their journey. This next barrier would give them the answer and possibly change the complexity of their Christmas festive season – maybe forever.

Meanwhile, Nessie was making good ground, which was totally a different journey going back home. Archie and Betty had gone back to their graves, and the two young children whom she'd fallen in love with were brought to the orphanage. Sadly, Uisdean had allowed his life to be taken in order to free Nessie to go back home with the golden egg, which could keep dinosaurs alive for maybe another century. She knew in her heart that she was fortunate to be heading back home to Scotland.

The Odessa authorities ventured on the side of financial gain from all the publicity. They decided to build a wall and a huge memorial where the monster was found dead. This would bring visitors to the area, and the main aim was to take the tourist trade from Scotland. After all, it was their monster that had caused all this. Let's not forget that blowing up the dam and all the submarines had cost a lot of money. The fee to see the memorial may not pay all the damages, but it would be some payback, and it would also sting the Scottish bed and breakfasts that had survived for many years on tourists coming to see the monster. They themselves didn't believe in.

Mary and Donald stood outside the blue-grey building, anticipating that their next move was crucial. As they walked the icy path, they could hear children laughing. They pressed the door bell and waited. This orphanage knew very well how often the doorbell would ring in a day, with children in distress. After a few moments, the door opened, and a woman in her mid-thirties named Natasha welcomed them and ushered them through a large hallway and to the seating room.

The woman realised that they weren't from the area. When you go to another country hoping to find your children, it is an issue you have to deal with very carefully. In their best English, the couple said they were here to try to find their children.

They were asked the name of their children, and Mary answered Hamish and Seonag. The woman shook her head and indicated that they did not have anybody with those names on record. The McPhee's looked at the woman with disappointment and sadness. The woman looked at them both and pointed to the wall containing all the pictures of children at the orphanage.

Mary went closer to the board and shouted, "These are my children! These are my children!" But to her horror, under the name of her son was Serge, and under her daughter was Luba. Donald joined her, and together they said, "Something must be wrong." They were so close to the children. Would they be denied meeting Hamish and Seonag? Why give them new names? This was too much for the tired couple, who had been on the road for eighteen hours.

The young woman knew she needed assistance, and so she excused herself and left the room.

Two days prior to their arrival to Odessa, the president of the orphanage, Dr Ramo, had a dream as clear as the one Nessie had in her palace. In fact, there may have been a connection. The dream showed him that the two children who'd arrived some time ago were special and were very different from the others. The dream also showed that one day their parents would come from another country to take them back home. When Dr Ramo woke up, the dream stayed very vivid in his mind. It confused him how anybody from a foreign country would come to take away the children. He thought no more of it and put his dreams down to fatigue from long hours preparing for the children's Christmas party.

The young woman reappeared with Dr Ramo following behind her. He had a broad smile, introduced himself, and offered some snacks and drinks to the couple. The four of them sat down around the little table. Mary and Donald explained that the two children on the wall were their children. Dr Ramo interrupted. "Where are you from?"

Donald quickly replied, "From Scotland," as if it was just down the road.

Dr Ramo politely said, "Welcome to our country." He then brought out a ledger containing pictures of all the children. "Are these your children here?"

Mary hysterically said, "I know my own children. I brought them into this world."

Dr Ramo asked them for their IDs, birth certificates, and any documentation that would prove the legality of their parenthood to these two children who were under his jurisdiction.

Mary and Donald looked at each other. They had nothing. It was very unprofessional to come with nothing, but Mary and Donald were unprofessional. Their hearts sank as they pondered the distance of their travel – which could conclude without seeing their children. Why were they brought here all the way from Scotland, just to be tormented because they couldn't produce paper documentation? It was time for Mary and Donald to listen. They hoped that the God of Grandma would help them. All their lives, their battles were won and lost by shouting and screaming. This time had to be different.

The couple was heartbroken and frustrated. With a heartfelt tone in his voice, Dr Ramo said, "I cannot give the children to you without presenting to me the documents. It would be totally illegal for me to do it."

Mary rose from her chair and was asked quickly sit down beside her husband. The conversation became more professional than at first. They now realised that they were not going to get the children without proving in some way they were the parents.

Dr Ramo paused for a moment and said, "I have a problem tonight. It is the children's Christmas party, and my Santa and elf are sick." He turned to Donald. "Mr McPhee, would you be so kind as to be our Santa? Your wife could be our elf."

Mary looked at her husband as if to say, "Would it help to get our children?"

Dr Ramo said, "This is the plan. When the children come to collect the presents from you, if these children, Serge and Luba –"

Mary raised her voice. "You mean Hamish and Seonag."

"If these children are really yours, they will recognise you as they come close to you."

There was silence for a moment. The McPhee s agreed. Everyone seemed settled and happy. They sat for a while as Dr Ramo laid out the plan for the party. The McPhee's then accepted some food and drinks.

"In fifteen minutes, the children will have played all their games and had their Christmas meal. The highlight of the evening is Santa and his elf handing out presents. For many children around the world, this is a yearly routine. Children take presents for granted. But the majority of these children have never experienced receiving a well-wrapped present. They read it from books and are told to them by other children speaking about Christmas, but its' not part of their lives.

Instructions were given to the McPhee's. They would go in where the Christmas tree was, and the children would be called one by one to receive their gifts from Santa. Nearer the end, they would see Hamish and Seonag come forward. This brought a smile to Mary's face: at last they would be calling their children. Dr Ramo held his cards close to his heart. He knew now that the dream was real, but he couldn't simply hand over the children as if he was selling food. His heart knew the code of practice for this situation.

The suit fitted Donald very well because he was stocky. Santa time can be very exciting for the children at a certain age, but in the Orphanage of Dreams, this was an exceptionally exciting time for the former street children.

The time was near for Santa to arrive. He had a bell

in one hand and a sack on his back, although most of the presents were already under the tree.

Doors opened wide, and they saw the bright lights of the Christmas tree and heard many children shouting excitedly. As Santa entered the door, there was great excitement. None of these children knew that Santa was from Scotland, and funny enough, the elf did as well. The children were asked to sit on the floor. Santa got closer to the tree, and Dr Ramo introduced the children to Santa and his elf, saying how pleased he was that they came to the orphanage on this very cold evening.

Each child came to Santa to collect their presents. Mary and Donald's eyes looked for Hamish and Seonag. But when children were cared for properly, dressed, got the best nourishment and proper sleep, and wore the best clothes, they looked like normal children. All the children were wearing Christmas hats. The lights were dimmed, and it was very hard to recognise their own children. As the line got smaller, Donald and Mary began to sweat. Maybe they weren't here and their minds had played games, especially when they had been on the go since the early morning.

A staff member called on Serge, and they called on Luba too. Serge had never seen Santa before, so he walked slowly. By this time, Luba had almost caught up with him. As Serge got closer to Santa, Donald knew his own son. He had to be patient for a few more seconds, and he remembered to follow the plan. As he handed over the present to Serge, the boy held it for a split second and then dropped it. Serge grabbed Santa and hugged him. This was no longer Santa – this was Daddy.

Luba never even got close to Santa; she had her present given to her by the elf, and she didn't wait to be given her present. It was the best Christmas present: her mom. All the other children stared in amazement, as well as the staff. Only Dr Ramo knew the whole story.

Beside the Christmas tree were two children and their parents, who had been separated by alcohol and then brought together by the grace of God. The other children got hysterical and started to clap; they knew something exciting was happening.

Dr Ramo had to intervene and instructed the children to be quiet. It was very hard to quieten the children, who had just got their Christmas presents and then saw the reality of a love affair of a family. Dr Ramo said, "This is a very special Christmas for you all, but for these two children, it's really special because their mom and dad have come to take them home." Scotland was not mentioned. He continued to encourage the other children that someday their parents would come and hopefully reunite their families. The McPhee family were led to the guest room, where the children were presented with the Christmas presents that Mary had brought in faith. The children spoke a foreign language and had foreign names, but these now had dispersed. Once again they had the Scottish names and their Gaelic accent. Outside the guest room, the other children soon forgot what had happened and were playing with their first toys from Santa. For the staff and Dr Ramo, this was the Christmas of all Christmases.

Nobody was in a hurry to start the next day, which was

Christmas day. Dr Ramo came to the orphanage and took the McPhee's to his own home for Christmas lunch. As the day went on, Mary had had a burden on her heart since the previous night. She knew that they would be leaving the country in fifteen hours. Would the children be coming home with them? They had no passports and no tickets. She cried in her heart. She didn't know much about jet-setting, but she knew that the children needed passports and tickets.

That evening they were invited to a carol singing in a church, and the singing was beautiful. Donald felt that something was bothering his wife. He knew that there was something missing. Everything had unfolded so quickly and turned out well beyond their expectations.

The world would not be so cruel to them that they would go home without their children – it was impossible. But Mary knew in her heart that she couldn't act like she had the previous night and demand the children. She felt that she had to be patient. The little she knew about God was enough that she would trust him in a time like this.

They came close to the end of the evening, and Dr Ramo stood up to speak. "Thank you very much for coming We greatly appreciate your presence and coming to church on this special day. We would like to wish the McPhee family, travelling to Scotland tomorrow, a safe journey." He asked two children from the choir to present the McPhee family with a gift. Mary was handed the gift. The custom was to open the present in front of everybody. Donald watched his wife with tears in his eyes as she pulled the wrapper away to find a beautiful family Bible. For some reason, she felt she wanted to open it. The bible was bulging in the middle. When she opened it, there were two passports and two tickets. They were placed in the fourteenth chapter of the book of John with a circle around verse 27. Mary smiled because she knew the verse very well. People clapped.

Most didn't know the love story behind the family's journey, where alcohol was once their master. The two innocent children had made a stand for sobriety, the deep love for their parents broke their hearts to the point of despair. It drove them to the other side of the world to get the fulfilment of Grandma's prayers for the family. Sadly, many a mother or grandma do not see their prayers fulfilled while with them, but years after they were gone.

28

CHRISTMAS WAS NOW COMPLETE FOR the McPhee's. They would soon board the plane for their beloved Scotland, the land of heather and midges.

Poor Nessie had no Christmas presents, no Christmas food, and no Christmas pudding. Well, she did have a bun in the oven – a saying for one carrying a child, which in this case was the golden egg.

It was a special Christmas for the whole world, which had been caught up with the story of Nessie. Even during Christmas, the world still spoke about it. Was it over? Was she dead? Would she turn up in Loch Ness? The excitement went on. Who would be home first, the McPhee's or Nessie? She was making good ground with no mishaps.

As the McPhee s rested in their beds the night prior to flying, they reflected on the whole story: two parcels through their letter box and crossing that ferry to their beloved island.

The McPhee family headed for the airport in Odessa after the best Christmas they'd ever had. It was always a good Christmas if one was away from one's children and then was reunited. Mary and Donald had only one thing on their minds: to arrive at Cruach na Moine.

The children were not aware of what had happened to them. Although they were heading for the plane, it was as if the children were on a timer, and each moment of life was a step closer to getting home. At this time, they were not aware of Cruach na Moine or Rex. All they knew was they were following the footsteps of their dad and mom, and eventually they would be okay.

They were strapped in the plane, and within a very short time, they were up in the clouds. There was no extra excitement for the children, and within a very short time, the two were fast asleep. When the children had left Loch Ness to go to Odessa, they'd slept most of their time in a trance. Here they were, high in the clouds, and they were fast asleep again!

It was the festive season, and so Mary and Donald had a special treat. The airline had laid on a special Christmas dinner for all the passengers. Donald and Mary were not used to this kind of attention, mostly because they'd never allowed themselves to mature like normal people.

It was brought to the passengers' attention that they would soon be landing in Glasgow. The children were wakened and were not quite sure where they were, and by the time they did, they were on the tarmac in Glasgow. Customs took the best part of an hour, and when they reached the entrance, they felt the cold breeze of Scotland. It was a short journey in a taxi to the bus station, where they would board for the four-hour journey to the island.

Away back at Cruach na Moine, Rex, who had been staying with a neighbour, got very fidgety and wanted to head for the door. For some reason the dog wanted out. He didn't want to eat or drink – he just wanted out. Old Callum, who was seventy-five, had looked after the dog as if it was his own. Eventually he gave into the dog's demands, and the dog headed for the bus shelter. Callum followed him, and the dog refused to move from there.

Eventually Callum lost the plot with Rex, and he called him stubborn and ungrateful. Poor Rex simply looked at him. The dog knew in his heart that his friends were on the way. Although he could not have gone with them, he knew they were coming back. He didn't hold any grudges, but he could sense there was going to be a reunion.

As the bus drove to the outskirts of Glasgow and into the hills of home, the children teased each other. All of a sudden, Hamish let out a shout. "We'll soon see Rex!" His face lit up with excitement that soon they would see their faithful friend once again.

They weren't sure when they'd seen him last, but when they did see him, it would be as if it was yesterday. That was the love affair they had with their faithful friend. Bit by bit, their memory was being allowed to come back enough to bring them into a lifestyle of sobriety.Within thirty minutes they would be crossing the ferry to the island

They came to a bus stop where several young people

who were intoxicated boarded. It was the festive season, and this did not bring memories to the children of seeing drunkenness; neither did it bother Mary or Donald. This happens if you have put something at the very back of your mind, and it is no more part of your future.

As the bus slowed down to board the ferry, Seonag let out a shout. "We'll soon be at Cruach na Moine." Their hearts started to pound when they remembered the green green grass of home. They had thoughts of school and their friends. They'd never had many. but since they'd stopped being bullied, life at school had been much better.

This was the road that Mary and Donald took many nights in their drunkenness, but tonight they were seeing it with clear eyes. There was excitement amongst the family; they had never done this before, travelling the bus as a family.

A mile from home brought them to the outskirts of the village. By this time, Rex had got the scent very strongly. He was up and down the road, making sure he was not too far from the bus stop. As the bus turned the corner, the bus stop was in view. Although Rex couldn't see the people, he knew his family was on it. The bus driver smiled; he knew the dog very well, and he opened the door. Rex didn't even look at the driver but ran to the back of the bus, to where the children were seated. He got very excited, and if he could speak, only words of love would come out. When they left home a long time ago, Rex was left at the gate, disappointed that he was not part of where they were going. That was done, and they had returned as if it had never happened. As adults, we could certainly take a leaf from Rex's book.

As the family walked up the path, the garden gate was no longer broken, the fence had been sorted, the windows were painted, and the grass was in good condition. This was a normal home not only on the outside but also on the inside. The children headed for their rooms while Rex following behind them, so excited he didn't know which room to enter. Mary prepared supper as the children prepared their clothes for school. The children were not aware how things had changed in their home; they saw it as if nothing had changed, just the alcohol. When this was removed, no matter how poor the home was, it would still be a happier one.

After supper, the children prepared their school lessons. Although it would be a few days before school, because they were still on holiday, they wanted to be ready. This would be the first time in a long time that they'd slept in their beds. They had slept at the shore of Loch Ness, slept in the belly of the monster, slept in an orphanage, and slept on the plane – but tonight it was in Cruach na Moine.

Donald and Mary sat together on their sofa, unwilling to speak openly about their travels. Not drinking alcohol and having their children back was enough to fill the void in their lives.

School holidays were over, and the children did what they did before. They jumped out of bed, went to the wash room, had porridge and boiled eggs, collected their school bags, and hugged their parents before leaving. This was part of the privilege of sobriety: everybody in the family got to be part of it. With their coats on, they headed out the door.

Donald and Mary stood at the window, watching their

children walk down the path with Rex behind them. Rex knew that it wouldn't be like before; they would return before sundown. Mary and Donald held each other. This was a moment to savour, a happy home. As the children disappeared round the corner, they realised how blessed they were. What happened today was not for a season – it was for a lifetime.

29

BUT WHAT ABOUT NESSIE? WAS SHE
dead or alive? According to world news, she had died
and was buried in a foreign country. Well, that's not the
Nessie I know.

The world tried to come to terms with the confusion
about who was buried in Odessa. Was it Nessie, or was it
her friend Uisdean? The only evidence of his existence was
the Scottish bonnet and a few fat maggots. Sadly, it looked
as if the world had accepted that Nessie was gone for good.
Like every top story on television and in the papers, a time
came when it was over. Film stars, great footballers, and
politicians all reached a point where they became history.
The media wanted something fresh. Was this the end of an
era regarding Nessie?

One thing was for sure: Odessa was getting much
publicity, and many tourists were going there to view the

memorial. Overall, this was a great concern for those who were dependent on the tourists who flocked to Scotland.

The people of Scotland obviously did not believe in Nessie, but still they were saddened with all the attention that was now focused away from them, in Odessa. Had they taken the story of Nessie too casually? Maybe they should have stopped to think that there may have been a glimmer of truth around the sightings – and maybe now they were getting what they deserved.

The hotels, bed and breakfasts, cruise boats, and souvenir shops were very unsure about their future. They'd had it good for many years, and now they may have to leave the shore of Loch Ness and look elsewhere to make a living. Never did they think that Nessie's fame would dry up. They also knew without Nessie, the potential to sell their business would be very hard.

Thousands had flocked to Loch Ness each summer. Not only the young but also many adults came from many countries around the world. For many, it was their second home, and they met many times and mingled with others from different countries. They kept in touch by letter, and many even got married. Relationships had started on the shores of Loch Ness.

They came from America, Japan, China, Malaysia, Australia, the Philippines, and all corners of Europe. It was a world meeting place, and people loved walking on the shore of Loch Ness, watching the sunset, and then seeing the sunrise the next day.

In America, a bunch of Nessie supporters decided to

make contact with all other supporters and those who visited the loch, to say goodbye to the land and to the lady of the loch. A fond farewell would be arranged. A date would be set in the springtime, a time when many would start their normal travels to the loch in the past. As news spread regarding the farewell, there was great interest throughout the world to attend. April 17 was the set date, and at sunrise of that morning, a ceremony would take place in the area where Nessie was last spotted.

Those in charge of the event had to gain permission from the landlords and had to involve police and security. In a short time, the Nessie followers were granted permission to go ahead with the event. This brought the press one more time, wanting to cover this last ceremony because they'd been previously involved from Loch Morar to Odessa. Prior to the event, some documentaries would be made regarding the previous life of Nessie.

There was total confusion about where Nessie was. Was she buried in Odessa? Who was Uisdean? These were questions that many people asked. When Nessie was just Nessie in the loch, it suited everybody, both those who believed and those who did not.

The good news for the locals was that they would be busy for two or three weeks, first with construction workers and then with the TV and news. Many people around the world wanted to take one last trip to the loch. The locals were confused about what was going on and kept their thoughts to themselves; as long as people came, they would spend money, and this money would have to do the locals throughout the winter. But three weeks would not be enough to cover the expenses over the winter months.

So many people wanted to attend that the fairest way was to issue tickets for the occasion. It would only be fair that the local people and the surrounding islands also got an allocation. A committee was set that would be in charge of the tickets for the event. One of the members of the committee visited Drumnadrochit to ask the locals if they were interested in attending the ceremony. Some jumped at the opportunity, maybe just to be nosy; others were not so keen.

When the council member approached the local garage, he spoke to the owner and asked if any of his colleagues were interested in free tickets. He smiled. "I will ask them." When he did ask, most laughed at him. But to their shock and dismay, Lachie came forward and asked for two tickets. His colleagues started to laugh and tease him. "You stopped drinking, you go to church, and now you believe in Nessie?"

A few days later, another council member visited the island to see if anyone wanted to have the few remaining tickets. He entered one of the stores that sold everything, and he was overheard speaking to the manager by Mary McPhee, who had been in the store. She abruptly barged in and asked for four tickets for her family. She got her tickets and headed home.

During supper that evening, she announced to her family that they were invited to a function of the island. The children jumped with excitement until they were told that it was a farewell for Nessie. Hamish piped up, "Who believes in Nessie? There's more chance of Scotland winning the World Cup than believing in her existence."

Seonag went to her room to get her Nessie toy, which she got when she's young. She told her mom, "This is as far as I believe in Nessie – a cuddly toy." If only they could focus on their past rollercoaster, unusual trip to the Orphanage of Dreams, as well as the sobriety of their parents.

Donald said nothing. He knew that there were things during the last few months which he could not put together regarding his children. How did they get to Odessa? And how was it that during this period, the Nessie story was in the papers and on television for weeks? He possibly would never put together the missing link. All he knew was that he had his children back.

With only a few days to go, the platform was almost completed. There was a large police presence to ensure safety, and security was brought in from Glasgow to control the large crowd. Many who had no tickets still intended to come. This was a farewell to a monster who had no real entitlement to a farewell, according to many. But the farther people were from Loch Ness, the more they intended to believe in the existence of the lady of the loch. Many from Scotland went to Florida to see Mickey Mouse, and many from Florida came to Scotland to see Nessie, so what was the problem?

The day before the event, the area was full of reporters querying the locals about what they thought of the fuss. There was very much a carnival atmosphere, and even the business people and the hotels relaxed and enjoyed the atmosphere. The makeshift campsite was filling very quickly, and people could smell the Nessie burgers, which were very popular with the children. There was a great possibility that they were simply normal burgers, but with the name of Nessie added, they tasted better.

The weather was favourable. It changed quickly in Scotland, up to three times in a day. Many would not go to bed that night and would party the whole night. This was going to be once-in-a-lifetime party, one that would continue until the last of the Nessie supporters flew home. Although this was a farewell party, many saw it as a wake.

The morning of the event, the McPhee's left early. Seonag and Hamish were glad to get a day away from the island, and very soon they were caught up in heavy traffic going to the same place. Donald and Mary were silent at the front of the vehicle, and their minds were set on the missing part of the lives of their children. Did this farewell gathering have anything to do with their children? Would they get satisfaction regarding their children being abroad?

The family knew there may be a connection between the missing monster and their children. It was something that their children could not be confronted with, and it was astonishing to think that just maybe the two young children were behind the disappearance of Nessie. This was so vivid in their minds because the whole world was coming together.

Hamish and Seonag were annoying each other, just like normal children. This was an emotional day for the McPhee's. What was more emotional was that they had to keep it to themselves, but there were times in people's lives that they had to keep secrets for the rest of their lives, and this was one of those times.

Miles away at Drumnadrochit, Lachie was with his wife, who'd agreed to come with him only to please him. Lachie, similar to the McPhee's, had his own secret thoughts regarding the young boy that had led him to shore of Loch Ness. It was during this period that Lachie stopped drinking and decided to follow God. His whole life had changed from that day, just like the McPhee's. He also could not share the secrets with anybody else.

On the road from Oban, a young married couple were making their way to Loch Ness. They would never forget their encounter with Nessie. She had changed their honeymoon and their lives, since the moment they'd promised to never go public with their encounter.

The stage was set, and the moment had arrived. The crowd was in place and was told via the PA system that the ceremony would start in seven minutes. The weather was beautiful, which was an asset to the ceremony. It was strange that the crowd had been quiet long before its start. On the platform were twelve personnel, seated. A lone piper played the tune over "The Sea to Skye" from the hilltop. The setting was beautiful, and within a short time, the sun would make its way up from behind the hills of Loch Ness. The calm weather was unusual, with just a small breeze on the lake.

A woman from Nigeria with an American accent, who lived in Ashland, Virginia USA, came slowly to the platform with a smile. This was not the smile of joy, but one of sadness. She indicated that her forefathers had come from Scotland.

The whole world seemed to tell people their forefathers came from Scotland. They wish.

She told of the sadness that surrounded the ceremony, adding that she had been coming for years to the shore of Loch Ness and was delighted that so many had taken the opportunity to come and share this last farewell to the lady of the loch. She went on to thank the local community, especially how they put up with foreigners intruding on their privacy. They accepted them as if they were neighbours.

She said, "Everybody in attendance must always keep in their hearts the great memories of the past regarding Nessie. You must not to leave the loch today with sadness, but with joy that you were part of something that will last forever, like a relative you may not see for days or years, but you still love them the same. This is the way it must continue. It is no secret that it will never be the same at the loch again. My family and I will come back occasionally, but sadly it's a long way to come just to see the scenery."

This was not what the bed and breakfasts and hoteliers wanted to hear. She went silent for a moment, as if to gather her thoughts with a lump in her throat. There was complete silence in the crowd. This was an emotional time, and the sun was about to rise. She indicated that she was fine. As she prepared to leave the platform, she introduced Mr Campbell from the isle of Barra, who had been sent to Odessa to identify the Gaelic code on the tartan bonnet.

A wee stocky man made his way to the platform. Mr Campbell had become a celebrity since his visit to Odessa and identifying the code that was on the bonnet. Was it a love story of parting for the last time, caused maybe by uisdeans sacrifice? They may never know. "What we really do know is that our Lord Jesus Christ went to Calvary to give his life for ours." This was his sacrifice for us.

As Mr Campbell was about to take the microphone, when there was a faint sound of music. Everybody looked around, but it wasn't coming from any specific area. One moment they thought it was coming from the hills, and the next moment it sounded as if it was coming from the lake.

They could hear it getting louder. It sounded Scottish, and it was emotional. In the distance, the sky turned red as the sun prepared to come over the hill. Children held their parents hands, and older people got closer to each other for a moment to savour. This was not part of the program. There was peace and tranquillity, as if everybody was waiting for something to happen. The music sounded as if it was gathering into one area in the lake. The skyline got brighter, and many now could identify the music that was being played by unseen musicians. It was first the beautiful tune called "morning has broken"the morning had just broken. "And the tune the skyline of Skye" was also played, this island was where the village of cruach na moine had stood.

The audience held their breath, and within a split second they saw the calm water begin to break about 500 meters from the shore, as if a squall of wind was concentrated on that area. In a breathtaking moment, the lady of the loch, Nessie appeared. There was no shout, no screams, just tears after all these years of waiting. By the time that thought entered their heads, she was gone.

The music got quieter, and the ripples in the water calmed. The whole loch went back to what it was several minutes earlier. Everybody kept staring. The music started to leave the loch and head to the hills. The music became faint until they could hear it no more.

"The music can be found on u tube,,,,,,,go to "Monster mania the love story of dreams The glen",,,,,,,, Is played by the author on harmonica."

There was no hysteria, just silence. One by one, everybody hugged each other as if to say, "I was there." Hamish and Seonag hugged each other. Lachie fell to his knees in tears. The honeymoon couple openly cried.

A well-dressed, tall man appeared from the crowd and made his way to the microphone. The proposed schedule was no longer in place. He made a motion for the crowd to be quiet, and within minutes there was silence. The American gentleman identified himself as the founder of one the biggest TV companies in the world, and he said how privileged he was to have been there for this moment, which may never happen again.

He said, "I believe she he's given us her real name for us: Maggie. I believe that this was for our eyes only. For us, we made the choice to come here with a kind of love, believing that Nessie was real. Do you really want to share your pictures with the world, sharing them with people who couldn't care less if Nessie is dead or alive? Many have come a long way – in fact, thousands of miles. Ask yourself, do you want to take home memories in your heart, or dead pictures that may have value only for others? True love is in the heart, not in pictures. "I have instructed my company to delete all the footage and all the pictures. I urge you to do the same. I can't force you to delete all your pictures."

There was silence in the crowd, and nobody shouted to object. Eight company producers of TV news also shouted they would delete all the film. Then hundreds of people shouted, "We have deleted!" Throughout the crowd and outside the fence, others said, "We also deleted."

There was a silence. Nobody wanted to leave and stared at the hills and the lake, where Maggie had come from and had performed the breathtaking music. Maggie's name was only for those who believed in her existence – what a bonus! But what astonished most of the people was that Maggie looked so young. Nobody in the crowd could tell that the golden egg had hatched. Only two little children knew, but they'd had their memories deleted. Uisdean was the unseen hero, who had given his life to allow this day to happen.

There was an announcement that the Nessie burgers were free. One didn't have to tell Hamish and Seonag twice, and they headed to the trailers to get their burgers. If the world only knew their involvement, they might have been entitled to double Nessie burgers!

The crowd dispersed very slowly. They all knew that it would take some time to leave the lake because of the traffic.

As Donald, Mary, and their children made their way to their vehicle, Donald nudged his wife and said, "Oh, there's the man from the garage, from where I ordered four new tyres." Donald shouted and called the name of Lachie.

Lachie heard him and stopped. He recognised Donald

and come over to speak to him. Donald asked him if his new tyres had arrived at the garage. Lachie went white because he recognised Hamish. He knew this was the little boy who'd come to the garage. Lachie didn't hear Donald as he was speaking about the event. Lachie was stunned. Was this moment evidence that the whole story of Nessie was real and that he was a part of it?

It was a part that he would always keep in his heart. He assured Donald that the tyres would be delivered the next week. Lachie then made his way to the car and asked his wife to drive. His mind could take no more, and it was only ten o'clock in the morning. He had satisfaction and peace in his mind, and he was so glad that his heart wasn't motivated to speak to the boy. Had the curtain now come down on Lachie's involvement? He opened the window of his car, took the nut from his pocket, and threw it back to the shore of Loch Ness, where it belonged.

This shocked his wife. "Why, Lachie?"

The McPhee's made it home by mid-afternoon. When supper was ready, it was well into the evening. Both children made their way to their rooms. Hamish started looking at the pictures they'd taken on the way to Loch Ness and the ones his parents had taken. To his horror, there was a picture of Maggie. Hamish said, "Why? I deleted just like the rest of the people." He tried deleting it again, but it wouldn't. Just then, he saw his door open slowly; it was Seonag speaking in a low voice so as not to be heard.

She said to her brother, "I deleted the picture of Maggie, but it's still in my camera. I have tried to delete it, but it stays." They looked at each other. "Are we meant to have this picture? We didn't break any law." Seonag returned to her room.

Although Nessie had cut ties with the children, she still wanted to protect them from a distance. This amazing story changed the lives of all who were at the ceremony forever.

As the children slept, Donald and Mary reflected on the day. They believed that this would be the day they stopped speculating on the missing months of the children. They simply wanted to move on and see their children grow in their sobriety.

The next day. Nessie was back in the headlines, but there were no pictures. The whole world believed in the existence of Maggie.

with everybody singing it in different languages. Possibly the loudest singing was at the loch side, where the bed and breakfast proprietors were having a ball; it was business as usual. They could see their winter holidays in the sun. What a day!

Back in Odessa, the authorities were stunned and believed somehow one or two monsters had pulled the wool over their eyes. Did one die so the other could live? Was that the reason why the little bonnet had changed the course of the whole story? Maggie was home. What about the memorial in Odessa? "Oops, let's not go there," they said. It was more embarrassing that she'd swum back through the waters of the secret submarine base. What a cheek!

Let's reflect on this fascinating journey of two children who were desperate to leave their addicted parents and so tried to make an impossible journey to the other side of the world. They made it with all the trials surrounding Nessie. The story has a happy ending.

When alcohol is removed from a family, it can have the same impact as Hamish and Seonag had. Will we ever know what relationship Maggie and Uisdean had?

Lachie continued to go to church, accompanied by his wife. The McPhee's never drank again. Donald became an elder in the church, and the children grew up not knowing their untold past. The honeymoon couple took a walk in the park with a set of beautiful twins. They would never forget the wonderful honeymoon with an intruder who was made welcome.

The story ends with everybody happy, even those from Odessa. Let's be fair: the whole world knew now where Odessa was. Of course, the world always knew where Loch Ness was: in the heart of Scotland.

The story closes with a truth from the author from Elgol on the Isle of Skye, just like Nessie. The woman from Nigeria had a dream in Ashland, Virginia USA at a Christian conference which Alister attended, that he would write a great book.When she confronted Alister he smiled politely and walked on, knowing that he was not capable of fulfilling this dream.

Twenty years on, the book was birthed with The grace of God nothing else, only grace Someday with God's grace, I may meet that wonderful Nigerian woman who met me that beautiful morning. She gave me her dream, and I ran with it. I was uneducated and had left school at fourteen years. I struggled with alcohol, but today I'm thirty years sober and am serving in the ministry. Who say there is no God?

To children who find themselves in the same situation as Hamish and Seonag: this was a story based on the dangers of alcohol in the family. Don't Run Away– stick with it. The tide of sobriety will come to your door. (if not always) a prayer will go a long way to bringing prolonged sobriety to your home. What God did for me, he will do for you.

I WAS ONLY A DRUNKEN FISHERMAN

I WAS BORN IN THE HEBRIDES OF THE west coast of Scotland, on the Isle of Skye. I was born in December 1949, the very month the revival spread through the Isle of Lewis and further afield. What is the revival, you may ask. It is when God pours out his spirit on all flesh. This happened when he heard the cry from his people, for the lost, and God answered.

I was brought up by my grandma in the village of Elgol, which looks across the Cuillin range of mountains with the islands of Canna, Rum, and Soay in the distance. My upbringing had no reflection on how I grew up in my later years. I wanted for nothing in a time when money was scarce. Being brought up in a Christian home is the best start in life for any child.

Leaving home for the first time has an element of excitement and fear, knowing that there were no restrictions when you came home in the evening, or whether you came home drunk or sober.

As I stepped from the ferry that brought me over the sea to Mallaig on the mainland, street lights and pavement were strange. My little village had neither of those. That first night, I looked across the water and wondered what my granny was doing. I was homesick and missed my grandma. I slept in a strange bed with no one to worry about me or to ask if I wanted a cup of tea. This was my first taste of loneliness.

At this point I pondered on my chosen career as a fisherman, not aware of the dangers I would encounter on the ocean. I had no thought of my battle with the swirling torment of booze that was ahead of me.

I recall one of my early days on the mainland, going for a drive one evening as the sun was setting behind the stretch of water called the Minch, which separates the inner and outer Hebrides. A local lad my own age asked if I wanted to go for a drive in his Ford Cortina Mark 2; this was the car of the time. The radio was on, playing a popular Frank Sinatra song, "Strangers in the Night". In the back seats were several young girls – everything a young boy with a sheltered life had dreamt of. To be honest, that was as good as it got. This was life without booze.

Within a few months, my lifestyle changed. I got into a culture that would have suited most teenagers: football, music, and drink allowed me to let my hair down, but I let myself down in the process.

This was an era few escaped. As fishermen, we crammed a great deal into two days ashore. The high seas with severe hangovers in bad weather were no fun. The skippers knew we were not pulling our weight; from the wheelhouse they could see the whole deck, we couldn't quit because we were hundreds of miles from land. By the weekend, after a good catch we were forgiven – until the next trip.

But a time came when I had burned all my bridges. I found myself jobless and homeless because the boat was my home. Skippers knew to avoid me, and eventually I ended up on a boat that found it hard to get a crew because they fished poorly. Basically, I was halfway to skid row.

My drinking life was quite normal. It started with a small portion of beer with 90 per cent lemonade. Sadly, this changed rapidly with less lemonade and more beer, until eventually it was 100 per cent beer. Eventually I was drinking spirits, which were stronger than beer. The buzz was great, and the feeling was new to me. My upbringing started to fade to the back of my mind. Bar activity was exchanged for my church life back home. This was not intentional; it simply happened. It happens to scores to young people today: the bright lights dazzle them, and the ethics of their youth are put on the back burner. It is so sad, especially when one has been there oneself. I feel deeply for them.

"I was good looking," which got me into a lot of bother. The swinging sixties was a time for wine, women, and song, and I certainly took my fair share. This lifestyle was only for a season, no matter how good and exciting. The time comes when the buzz wears off, and you realise that the mountaintop party is only for a very short period. For the rest of your life, you try to reach that pinnacle again; sadly, you never will.

The swinging sixties only lasted a short time in my life.

When booze took its grip in my life, I felt like sixty. My happy-go-lucky nature changed to a life of struggles.

My outer appearance changed. My ability to work dwindled to a walking pace. My ability as a good worker helped me a little, but I was unreliable and let down others. Was it time to move on? It's the place, it's the people, and it's the weather. Until you make up your mind to stop drinking, booze will follow you to your next watering hole. When I needed a drink in the morning, that was a sign that I'd reached a serious level. The worst was yet to come.

For the first time in my life, I encountered severe withdrawals that frightened me – but after a few days, I would improve and then go back drinking again. While I was on a bender, my grandma died. She was all I had, and she never had the privilege to experience my sobriety.

One Sunday evening while returning to my fishing boat, I fell over the side. I managed to hold on to the side until a crew member heard my cry and pulled me to safety. As I waited to be rescued, the radio, which was on in the wheelhouse, played "Amazing Grace". I believe God had a hand in my rescue.

This fear did not stop my desire to continue to drink. I continued to be a slave to booze. By my mid-twenties, I looked like an old man but believed someday I would overcome the slavery to drink. I experienced my first of thirty times in a mental hospital. When you reach that level in your life, you seem to get a stamp that sticks with you for many years, sometimes forever.

Was death round the corner for me? Surely not. I was

young and was entitled to a good time. Wasn't it part of being young? I only drank heavily. I caused no one any harm. Where was the sin? I didn't steal and wasn't violent. But guilt gave me many nights of restless sleep.

My years in the village of Mallaig were coming to an end. In those years, there was a dear woman who I believe was a nun. I will always remember her name for her kindness, compassion, and concerns for me. She was called Lizy Ann and was a Catholic. I found it strange because I came from a Protestant island and had no dealings with Catholics. This dear nun changed my outlook and thinking. She showed me what the Bible speaks about: love your neighbour.

Sadly, I made wrong decisions in my personal life while there, which I regret today. If only I could turn back the clock. But there are grounds you cannot go over again.

2

THE TIME HAD ARRIVED FOR A NEW start in life. I decided to head to Aberdeen in Scotland, where the oil industry was booming. Jobs were plentiful, and the money was good.

Working on the oil rigs was a dream job, with two weeks working and two weeks of holiday every month. Hitting the bottle again was always going to happen. A new environment did not change the cravings. The guys around me soon found out that I wasn't a normal drinker. Not turning up to fly to work offshore was a major problem. Companies lose faith in slackers, and eventually they are released from their contracts.

I was flying to an oil installation with a hangover, knowing it would be two to three weeks before I could get any alcohol. I knew before I dried out, I would have nightmares, panic attacks, and mood swings. I could not quit because I was broke. I was in a no-win situation. Sadly, once I started to recover, eating and sleeping was a sign I was ready for another bender. This went on till I was fired. It was a vicious circle that could have lead to death or close to it.

For a large part of my drinking life, I tried to look the sober guy. Everybody thought I didn't have a care in the world. I was always laughing and loved music and parties. Most of my friends went home at the end of the night, but not Alister. I needed more to help him sleep, and I needed alcohol to be motivated in the morning. What an existence.

In my late thirties, I was involved in a hit-and-run accident that resulted in my being in and out of hospital for two years. At the time of the accident, I was due to go to Saudi Arabia to work, but because of the accident, I was unable work for a long time. A large payout from insurance gave me the financial freedom to spend and drink big. While drunk, I bought a catering business. This was great because I was now a businessman who employed several staff. I had a sports car and a Jeep. Many people would give their right arms to be in my position, but sadly with poor management skills, heavy drinking, and rising debt, I was on skid row in less than eighteen months.

It's hard to believe how quickly you hit rock bottom. I remember the moment I was broke: a cold winter morning, alone. Being broke is one thing, but debt mounting up is even more painful. All I had worth selling was my jacket. What a choice: freezing to death in the cold or selling my jacket to buy booze. An hour in my fancy car with the heater on would have been nice. Of course, the car had been sold days earlier.

Why am I telling you this? To prevent it from happening to you. There's no other reason. Booze will take the coat off your back – literally. It did that to me. I thank God for making me laugh again, but I must never forget that once I cried.

3

DURING THIS TIME, I WAS DIAGNOSED with cirrhoses of the liver, and if I didn't stop drinking, I would be dead in two years. This was a serious blow to my mental health. Eighty thousand pounds in debt with two years to live, and I was homeless outside of my family island. Still, there were many others worse off than I in the world. A blind man was once asked whether there was anything worse than being blind. He paused for a moment and answered, "Yes. Sight without vision. There are thousands in the world today with no vision."

This is the first time I ever made it public that I suffered from bulimia and depression. Both of these mixed with booze made a dangerous concoction for suicide. I'm glad I wasn't weak enough for that.

Where were my drinking friends and those to whom I lent large sums of money? The long, lonely days in the hospital gave me time to reflect on the wasted years. I was an embarrassment to my family, especially on a closely knit island where everybody knew everybody.

Where did I go from here? The pub to drink and drown my sorrows. It was all I knew. I was a very sad man with no vision.

My circle of friends dwindled to just a few. When your money is gone, only close friends will stick by you. When I travelled to visit my family on Skye, a well-known gentleman would stop his car when he saw me, drunk and unclean. Instead of scolding me, he took me to his home, cleaned me up, fed me, and put me in the same room as his son. He did this many times. He was known as Painter Bob.

He was well known for his work with people like me. He never gave up on me. The very day he was buried, I quit booze forever. He had a way of telling me where alcohol would take me, and he pulled no punches in his guidance for maintaining sobriety. You really need a man like this to put fear in you regarding the dangers of how booze can not only damage you but also take your life.

One Sunday night around 7.00 p.m., as I drank alone in a bar with few people around, I felt convicted regarding my past life and wasted years. Weeks earlier, I'd found a tattered Bible. I hid it in the cistern of the toilet in the bar, and I read it several times a day. Many ask what I saw that night. When conviction brings you to despair, this can only be replaced by an overpowering presence of the Holy Spirit. For me, that Sunday I was urged to leave and enter a nearby church. One minute a large whiskey was in my hand, and the next I was standing at the altar of God, pleading forgiveness.

Long-haired, dirty, and scruffy, I knew I had an opportunity to turn my life around. I had to make the choice to accept or reject Christ. This is when faith kicks in. If you are waiting for flashing lights, you will be there all night. When the service was over, I was given literature, which I brought back to the bar. With a drink in one hand and gospel material in the other, for some reason the alcohol did not have the same effect; it tasted rotten. Drinking and I were about to separate for the last time. Two spirits cannot live in the same body – the spirit of booze and the spirit of God. It's impossible. Remember that, guys. The time had come when I laid it down for the last time.

I remember the hour I poured my booze down the sink with my wife watching me. I turned away that night and had no craving the next morning. I believe if I left the booze without pouring it till the morning, the craving would still be there. Now, thirty years on, I have never craved a dram, Scottish terminology for a whisky. Someone asked me was there any happy moments in my drinking days,I said yes when someone bought another bottle.

As my life of sobriety began to take shape over weeks and months, I saw the sunrise from a different angle. The adjustment was very hard. Responsibility was a new thing to me. Going to church every Sunday and helping others who were in my position was a great achievement for an ex drunk working in SunnyBrae alcohol Rehab Aberdeen, where I was once was a patient. I was living the dream of sobriety.

After a few years of marriage, my wife took sick and required a major operation. Sadly she didn't come through. She was my wife and my best friend, and then she was gone. Try filling that space. To explain grief would take up a large part of my short life story. A few months later, my mum died, as did my close friend. When there is an empty void in your life, you need to fill it with something different very quickly, or you will start to go backwards in a short time. All the excuses to go back to drinking would return.

It was hard coming home from work knowing the loneliness that was before me.On many occasions i would come home to find soup or a meal on my doorstep,this went on for months until I got stronger . Strangely the parents of the woman who left the food attended the church I met my wife .This was God grace supplying all my needs.

4

GOING BACK TO BOOZE WAS AN option. But we have a choice in life. In this valley of experience, God was not about to leave me on my own. Just like the footprints in the sand, he lifted me, set my feet on a rock, and established my way.

I had an opportunity to go to the eastern block, work with street children, and help a doctor who was building an orphanage. The doctor was grateful of any help I could give. Bless him. This was a great challenge and was very demanding, seeing others that were worse off than I was.

As you have gathered, the book is based on two children leaving Scotland to find the orphanage of dreams. The idea began with my travels to work with street children, my work in the fishing industry, and my years on the oil rigs. My awareness program point out the pitfalls to where alcohol can lead you. The documentary was real regarding my work overseas. My life is sewn throughout the book, pausing with a few nuggets to explain how I dealt with booze and finding Christ. Just like the children, I had a happy ending. I have showed the world through the book what alcohol does to a family, how booze can leave the fridge empty, and how it can create poorly nourished children. This is a huge world problem that is not being confronted by governments. Let's not forget that booze is big money for our country. Licensing laws have to change in order to save lives! The oil city of Aberdeen Scotland can live without oil, but it cannot live without alcohol.

I had an opportunity for a job in Arizona as a freelance Thermioligy engineering consultant – not bad for a drunken fisherman. The heat of Arizona was too severe for me, and eventually I was transferred to Ohio. It was while I was there I met my second wife, Janet. We married within a few weeks of meeting. I joined her in a Bible college in Marietta, Ohio. I studied there for almost four years, leaving with a pastoral degree. The president of the college saw something in me many others didn't see, and he awarded me with a free four-year scholarship. We also received two awards for our work in the community and with the prisons.

The opportunity to work in many prisons and rehab centres across many states was a godsend. Being part of an international choir was living the dream. We went from state to state to packed churches, I believe America gave me my life back. Today, I preach the gospel across Scotland, Asia, and Europe.

I recall one day entering a woman's prison in Ohio with

a picture of an inmate's daughter; it was given to me by her relative. I walked the line of twenty women, who were behind a glass panel. I could speak to them by intercom. I moved from panel to panel until one of the inmates cried that the photo was of her daughter. I helped her spiritually and brought her food and books. Sadly she had to do her time to get her freedom.

How fortunate I am to have lived a life of sobriety for thirty years. I worked in rehab centres, taking seminars and showing those who were less fortunate than I the dangers of addiction. This is where I get my satisfaction, seeing someone recover from booze and find Christ. There is no financial payment to merit this.

In 2016 I set up the North Sea Garden Mission to help the offshore men and women be aware of addiction. The North Sea Garden Mission (gardenmission.org) is a lighthouse to the lost. I thank Christ for giving me the opportunity to serve in this capacity. I urge you to spend time on this site. It carries the blueprint to sobriety and the stepping stones that will lead you to the saviour.

I believe God removed the addiction from me with much prayer. He killed the spider in my addict life. However, I had to deal with the cobwebs of my life. Dealing with debt and family matters is our responsibility.

Anyone who has followed my program with all his or her heart has maintained sobriety and grasped the plan of salvation.

At sixty-seven years old in 2017, I still roam the oil rigs, working and presenting my passion for Christ and putting forth the message of sobriety. If one person can find Christ or one person quits booze, then it was worth setting up this program. I reflect over my life and see the beauty of God shining through it.

My grandma, a nun, and gentleman Bob didn't know each other, but God did. How fortunate I was to have mentors like them.

My biggest challenge was writing this book. This only happened when an African woman told me she dreamed of me writing a great book. Twenty years on, God has given me the platform and the inspiration to write. I had left school at fourteen with no education, but I feel this can inspire others who were misfits.

After I lost thirty years to booze, God gave me back the years the locusts have eaten. God will forgive my past as if it never existed. That shows me the power of the cross of Calvary. This part of the book is not fiction but gospel.

It's just like Hamish and Shonag, who went the extra mile to find the orphanage of dreams. For us to get eternal life, we need to go from the natural to the supernatural and find Christ on our knees. Then we can find a good, strong church with a God-fearing preacher and a King James Bible under his arm. With the world behind you and the cross before you, there's no turning back.

Being a child of God is the pinnacle we all should strive to achieve; just like Nicodemus, we must be born again or converted.

Grasp your life with both hands, and push beyond the mark of the high calling. I remember my first drink at fourteen on the Isle of Skye, and my last drink in Aberdeen, Scotland, thirty years ago. I attained sobriety against the odds. If I can do it, you can give sobriety a chance.

"I HAVE FOUGHT A GOOD FIGHT, I HAVE FINISHED MY COARSE, I HAVE KEPT THE FAITH. (II TIMOTHY 4:7) KJV

For God so loved the world, that he gave his only begotten son, that whosoever believeth in him, should not perish, but have everlasting life. Amen. (John 3:16 KJV)

(If you do what you have always done, you will be what you have always been).

ADDICTION HELP LINE
psalm24v34@yahoo.com

This is where the author played as a boy, in Elgol on the Isle of Skye Scotland.

Lightning Source UK Ltd.
Milton Keynes UK
UKOW06f1609091217
314143UK00005B/221/P